D0935513

EARTHJACKET

Also by Jon Hartridge

BINARY DIVINE

EARTHJACKET

JON HARTRIDGE

WALKER AND COMPANY

New York

First published in the United States of America in 1970 by the Walker Publishing Company, Inc.

Library of Congress Catalog Card Number: 71-130810

Printed in the United States of America from type set in the United Kingdom.

ISBN: 0-8027-5532-1

EARTHJACKET

I

THE substance of the fleeper yielded deliciously as I landed and prepared to bound another thirty feet. With a movement that was a triumph of collaboration between brain, bone, muscle, sinew, nerves and machinery, I hurtled outwards and upwards at an angle of thirty-six degrees, manipulating its ears as I went.

I looked round to see her. I loved to watch her handle a fleeper. She was following close behind on her machine. Hers was blue, iridescent in the light, shining against the greenery and bright even against the sky.

Her hair rose from her shoulders and fell again, slow and heavy, and her bosom worked in contrariety to her motion, globular on descent and pendulous once more as she lifted off the ground. Her eyes shone with delight and there was a sheen upon her flawless skin that made her appear almost luminous as she hovered capriciously in a beam of light that took her fancy.

I sighed, and moaned a little with joy and led her out over the water stretch, across to the island. I liked riding a fleeper upon water best of all. There was a smack as it hit the surface and a slurp as it came away again that was pleasing to the ear. Taking off was accompanied by a slight dragging that never came to anything, but gave you thrilling little danger signals.

We had been round the valley that morning, up on the slopes, through the hanging-fields and down on to the munching-grounds; up to the bare slopes again and back to the plainfields by the edge of the running water. We had skimmed over the tops of the tangles and dodged through the pillar clusters, feeling the breeze on our bodies and the

5

warmth on our faces as we bounded across the territory.

There was no one to see us this time.

And now we were going to the island to pick the succulents and to drink the juice and to swim and to climb and to be close to one another.

'Smack-sloop . . . smack-sloop . . .' we went and I could hear her laughing.

When you rose above the water about ten feet you could see the silver shapes darting in among the greenstuff and the stones on the lake bed. The water was not deep and remained clear always.

We landed close together on the island's gravel beach and rolled off our fleepers and lay on the warm stones. I closed my eyes against the brilliant ceiling. There was a little noise and then her hand was in mine.

'Putputput . . .' The fleepers skittered away and stood together about twenty yards from us, one blue, one orange, perfect ovals, their ears rotating anxiously, as though awaiting a distant summons.

Soon they would be still.

I had never been quite sure how they worked. They were my own invention.

'Clever,' she whispered, coming closer. Her flesh, soft here, hard there, brushed mine. I felt a warmth inside. Our limbs entwined.

Rolling away I got to my hands and knees, then stood. I walked to the ladder cluster and climbed up to the succulents.

'Catch!'

We spat the little hard bits at each other and ran laughing to the water to wash and splash.

I ran until the water was above my knees. I heard her sudden shriek of laughter above the roar of the tiny waves about my head as I fell.

I turned and sat, washing the sweat and the sticky remains of the meal from me. She came beside me and did the same. Then she threw water into my face.

Blinded momentarily, I squeezed my eyelids tight and as I did so I somehow saw her clearer than ever, with her oval, olive face with just a hint of a blush at the cheekbones, heavy, honey hair falling on to slim shoulders, tawny eyes with a suggestion of green in them, a nose too broad and not straight enough for perfection, a generous mouth almost too ready to smile.

Shaking the water from my eyes I rose, bellowed, and gave chase.

I caught her in the shallowest part and pulled her down. We lay there, almost on the shore, in no more than an inch of water, she looking up and I looking at her eyes.

'The ceiling,' she said. 'It's got a crack in it.'

And as I laughed, I knew it was the truth and felt queasy. I rolled over and stared upwards too.

What had been blue perfection a minute previously was now dissected by a hairline fault.

'Ah no, please no, it isn't over!'

But the crack grew wide enough to permit the entry of a scream. She faded and fell away and the crack grew teeth and I found myself looking into a universal maw. The great tongue lashed in an ecstasy of greed and the palate shivered with excitement.

The surface on which I was lying recoiled leaving me suspended for a second before I crashed.

The mouth must never, never take me. I shuddered and shook my head to shake away the sight of it.

Above me was a handhold. I stretched up and felt with my fingers. They touched flesh. There was a groan and my fingers scampered away to seek the hospitality of inanimation.

Finding the plastic bar, I gripped and heaved. Standing there, wavering in the blackness, I tried and failed to see. And as I stood and shivered I heard the pattering of spilt pills. But I listened with the back of my mind and I didn't care about the pills.

I had to get away. The desire for escape overcame all others. Taking tiny, rapid, sideways shuffling steps my feet followed a route parallel to that of my fingers above, feeling their way along the rails.

Stop.

Right turn. Stop. Stretch. Another, as I thought there would be. Altogether six and then a wall.

My brain sensed that my body was shaking, but the vibration was something external, over which I had no control.

My knees had trouble in supporting me as I crept, arms before me, along the wall.

My hands wandered across great mountains and valleys and through great rivers of condensation as they felt their way over the rough and slimy wall; my feet crossed a continent of flooring before I found the door.

I found the door but not the release lever. Like a pair of blinded madmen my hands circled the surface as I searched for the device that would allow me to escape.

Escape! I found the lever and wrenched and heaved and found steel bands around my heart as my lungs rose and fell in inadequate endeavour. The lever would not budge. In defeat I sank to my knees. As I went down my right hand discovered a bolt and withdrew it and suddenly I was on the outside.

Greedily, I gasped and snatched at the atmosphere and found some relief.

But the fear was still with me, although the door had closed behind me with a solid thud and the hiss that denotes the making of a good seal.

The sky, now dimly lit and grey where the paint had peeled off, was no comfort. I felt once more as I had when I was in that blackened, airless room. The pursuit of me was not over.

I ran. And my breath shrieked noisily to smother the echo of my steps along the street. I could not, could not stop running and the people I passed stepped carefully out of my way. I pounded on, past the incurious old man I saw out of the corner of my eye just sitting there, past doors and roads I had never been past before.

I approached a large window that you could see into and

inside it was the image of a running man. The running man was I! The crowd-control cameras were following my progress with their lenses, passing me from one to the other as I ran in panic along the streets.

Thenceforth at every intersection where there was a screen my enlarged image would loom up at me, pass me by and recede before being picked up by the camera ahead.

I tried dodging down alleyways, turning on my tracks and back again: I tried everything but stopping. But wherever I went there was a camera in position to watch me.

The sight of me running, running, pursued my vision. I could escape neither from my fear nor from myself. I was running and my trap ran with me.

Now I could see myself running towards the screen again, huge-eyed, head lolling, staggering. I could not go much further. And the fear was still close behind.

He was out of control, this man on the screen. He ran without direction. His face, recently deep red, was now ashen. He could hear a peal of bells as he took the last, sluggish step, threw up his arms, and fell to the ground. The breath whistled and rasped in and out of him, desperately trying not to stop for ever.

Soon after, they came to pick him up, this wretched running creature. They moved slowly, with the minimum of effort. Their voices wheezed and they rolled him on to their wagon.

'He'll run no more.'

'No,' they said to each other. This did not make them amused. This did not make them sad. They simply observed.

The cart trundled softly along the quiet streets. He fought to remain conscious, for the fear was lurking there in his sleepstate. He failed, but the fear stayed away this time.

Then there was peace. I was lying in a white room, dim and quiet. I drew breath slowly and gently.

'One inhalation every thirty seconds. No more,' said the man on the screen above me. My lung power was insufficient to allow me an audible reply.

'It's the law,' he said. 'You consumed thirteen days' supply of respirable atmosphere between leaving the dormy and coming here. That includes,' he added softly, 'the amount consumed by those who were sent out to deal with you and the amount I am obliged to consume addressing you. So as a result you will be required to spend twenty-six days on half consumption.'

He closed his mouth and his eyes and remained still for a minute to recover himself.

'You may state your case,' he said. 'But this requires the convening of a committee of three. You will have to compensate for the air they consume during the hearing and, of course, you will have to go on full oxygen too, which will be forfeit should the hearing go against you, which it almost certainly will. So you would be well advised to go no further.'

He paused again, luxuriating in the full strength atmosphere. MY atmosphere! Bought with MY time.

'You may think about it. I shall return in twenty-four hours. You will let me know your decision then.'

The man disappeared from the screen. He had given me twenty-four hours to consider the statutory offer. You needed time to think on half-oxygen.

Breathing half-strength atmosphere was not physically distressing when one was medicated correctly, as I had been, but it slowed everything up – including the brain.

Some people enjoyed thinking at half speed. I loathed it. I hated the discipline of having to set half-thoughts aside while pondering their corollaries; fumbling at the back of my mind in amongst a fugitive and sluggish memory.

But I set my unwilling brain in pursuit of the problem I had set it.

He had advised me against appealing. Why? The law said I could. It was not, I decided, because it was against *my* interest but because it was against *his*. He, as a Texec, was commissioned to keep the peace and safeguard the happiness of the people.

But in my case he and his kind had failed.

The dream they had sent me was supposed to have promoted content. Instead it had driven me wild with fear. My presence in this cell was proof of their failure, not mine.

He should be punished, not I!

He, not I. . . . The enormity of my thoughts was breathtaking. I began to laugh at my own impudence, but the effort was too much.

Instead, I slept, without dreaming. My mind was evacuated, and the fear had gone.

But at the end of the twenty-four hours I was beginning to feel the first symptoms of oxygen starvation. The drug was wearing off. I could elect either for a further dose or . . .

He came on to the screen again.

'Do you wish to appeal against the statutory deprivation?' he asked, his lips moving only slightly as he uttered the words.

I raised my right index finger, signifying that I wished to appeal. His eyes closed, his nostrils whitened and his lips disappeared into a thin blue line.

'Very well,' he said. 'In another eight hours time.'

Instantly the bonds about my thorax loosened themselves, my throat's constriction was eased and the rigour gripping my limbs eased its hold as the hiss of the atmosphere exchanger filled the cell with sound.

I breathed deep and vigorously and my head spun as the full-strength atmosphere was sucked down into my lungs and coursed through my body.

A fury suddenly welled up within me. Why should I not always feel like this? Why should a man be born to suffer from an inadequate supply of the air he breathed?

It was said that the conditioning machines were working permanently at full capacity. That they were designed to supply a smaller population than ours. That they would be overloaded until such time as the race halved its numbers.

Well, what were we to do about that? Die?

I found myself pacing around the little cell. Never before in wakestate had I experienced such emotion, such a sense of purpose.

This was because a high-oxygen atmosphere was being let into my cell. It was a rule that in the interests of justice all parties to a dispute should be awarded a maximum supply of oxygen during and immediately before a hearing.

I resolved that I would in future fight against going on half-oxygen – and die fighting if necessary. And I promised myself that I would spend as long awake each day as I chose, and that I would take a Texec's share of nutriment each day. My only problem was the fulfilment of this resolution.

And then I realized that I had no problem. For I would just take what I chose. No one would stop me…would they?

This time, in escaping from the burdens placed upon me by my society, I would not simply run until I fell from exhaustion and thus deliver myself to it once more – I would match force with force and cunning with cunning and the technological might of the Texecs with . . . with a metal bedleg!

Triumphantly, I turned the cot on to its side, scattering the mattress and bedding over the floor. Gripping one leg with both hands I twisted with all my strength, rejoicing in my new-found stamina.

The sweat was running down me before the leg gave, first by a hairsbreadth, then by a millimetre, then by a quarter turn, a half turn as the thread was unwound from the socket.

When finally the bed yielded its iron leg I stood, feeling the weight of the club in my hand, thumping the mattress experimentally.

Then I explored the cell, examining the atmosphere ducts let into the bare white walls, checking the hermetic door for a sign of weakness. There was none. I tapped the floor to see whether or not there was an area of hollowness

12

underneath, prised up one tile, peered underneath and replaced it.

My examination of the cell yielded nothing of promise, yet I was still strangely full of hope. I was still incapable of recognizing the euphoria activated by a full-strength oxygen atmosphere; later I would be able to deal with this weakness as it appeared.

I screwed the leg back on to the bed, not too tightly, stood the bed upright again, replaced the mattress and bedding and lay down relaxed to await my inquisitors.

I did not have very long to wait. My eight statutory hours for pre-hearing deliberation were nearly at an end. I hoped that they had not been observing me. It was unlikely. What possible mischief could I get up to within the confines of a retribution cell?

As I lay there waiting, I suddenly remembered that my stumber pill was overdue. I felt in my pocket, but they were all gone. I recalled then that somewhere, sometime, I had heard them spilling on the floor.

I felt a twinge of dread and then, in the oxygen-induced optimism of the moment, felt that their absence was a blessing. (So it was, but for reasons I could not possibly appreciate at the time.)

'Hullo,' I said. He winced slightly.

'As you know,' he said, 'we are here to hear your plea in response to the charge that you consumed or caused to be consumed thirteen days adult ration of respirable atmosphere within forty minutes on the day before yesterday. I take it that you are not disputing the facts?'

'Certainly not,' I said. 'I will argue extenuating circumstances.'

'Then argue them,' he said.

'Very well. My case is that the dream machine was at fault. An error in the programming, or circuit eccentricity, what you will, caused me to experience powerful fear stimuli while under narcosis. I was not in control of myself.'

He came nearer to a smile than I had thought possible. 'It

13

is insufficient to claim, or even to prove, lack of self-control,' he said. 'Indeed, such an argument might lead us to the conclusion that it would be desirable for you to be permanently under surveillance in a half-oxygen institution . . .'

'That's not fair!' I shouted.

'Fair or not, society here in Lemington must be protected,' he said. 'But if I may be allowed to continue, your plea of no control is insufficient . . .'

I interrupted again. 'I must prove total automatism. Of a non-recurring nature, of course.'

Again the mask almost slipped. But this time he did not nearly smile. He nearly scowled. I had startled him. 'Quite so,' he said.

'In that case, I must call a witness. Here, to my place of examination,' I said.

Even now I don't know what made me say it, although I have a shrewd idea. But at the time, the words meant far more to him than they did to me.

He rose from his seat, his left hand squeezed tight against his side. He was an awful colour. I couldn't help sniggering. He sat down again. The men on each side, who so far had remained still and impassive, put their heads close to his.

'We cannot deny . . .' said one before they turned off the sound.

They conferred before me in mime. It was not hard to follow the drift of their conversation. They were sympathizing with each other, but they could not gainsay my right to a witness, to be presented at a place of my own choice.

They stopped talking. The principal inquisitor shook his head sadly as though to himself.

They turned on the sound link once more.

'Very well,' he said. 'Name your witness.'

For an instant, I could not reply. I had been so pleased with my unconscious stratagem that I had not considered who the witness could be. And then I thought. Perfect.

'Ferguson B,' I said. 'Section 44a, Precinct Omega.'

'He will be with you in three hours,' he said.

'Suppose he's asleep?' I said.

14

Again he turned a nasty colour. 'All right. We will recon-
vene within eighteen hours. We want to get this business
completed as soon as we can,' he said, giving me a look
which said plainly that the sooner he could consign me to
a lifetime's half-oxygen on reduced nutriment, the better he
would be pleased.

2

During that time in my cell, all that I saw of the world
outside came to me through an electronic screen which
woke and became dormant again at the bidding of another.
It was as though I, rather than the screen, were being activated and de-activated at the will of an outsider.

The peremptory disappearance of my inquisitors made
my solitude absolute. For the first time in my life, so far as
I knew, I was alone.

I unscrewed the bedleg and held it firm. It made me
feel less vulnerable.

To place me compulsorily in solitude was, perhaps, their
way of lowering my resistance. Their kind was always warning the likes of me how we were incapable of tolerating
change, of how an alteration in our routine was liable to
cause us psychic damage. We needed them, the strong
Texecs, to protect us and to order our lives for us, to see
that we came to no harm.

I had accepted this, like all the others, but I now saw it
for the lie that it was.

For here I was, alone and never so alive. And my
solitude allowed me to consider myself in a way that I
never had before.

It was a contented enough existence in its way. I slept
my statutory sixteen hours every twenty-four. During this

sleepstate I was refreshed (usually) by the dreams they sent me, and well prepared for the greyness of my eight hours awake, devoted to eating, working and physical regeneration.

Like everybody else, apart perhaps from the Texecs who were in control, I lived two lives. One asleep, one awake. We had all been taught that the one life was real and that the other was unreal. But most of us were uncertain about which was which.

But I knew which was which when they brought Ferguson B in.

As though for the first time I noticed the dullness of his skin, the dimness of his eyes, his dejected deportment, his sluggish movements. All this I took in as he was dragged through the door by a pair of guards.

I saw him, and thus myself, as though for the first time. If I had entertained doubts about what I was to do, it was his appearance that finally dispelled them. I had no desire to look like him ever again. I would rather die.

Quickly I pushed the cot on its three legs into the aperture left by the opened door and slugged one of the guards with my bed leg. He clasped both hands behind his neck, bowed his back, staggered a couple of paces forward, and tripped over the bedding to lie curled up on the floor, moaning. His companion ran away from me, found himself trapped in a corner and looked around him desperately, saw no prospect of escape from this extraordinary violent creature confronting him and began to whimper.

Triumphant I turned to the screen, preparing to smash the images of my three horrified inquisitors, when I realized that the cot was being squeezed by the heavy door which a powerful motor was trying to close.

Turning, I ran forward and leapt on to the cot and then jumped out into the corridor.

Then I saw Ferguson B again standing there in the middle of the chaotic cell, his face a numb mask of bewilderment.

'Oh, come on Fergy!' I said, and to his credit he tried

16

to. It must have been the residue of the full strength atmosphere in the cell that fortified his resolve.

He tottered towards the creaking cot and climbed on to it and fell there. He tried to scramble towards me on his hands and knees. The iron of the cot groaned as it was warped by the door. The springs sang as they were released one by one.

The gap was little more than eighteen inches now and still shrinking. Ferguson stretched out a hand to me. Considering his appeal for a fraction of a second before deciding, I reached out to him and heaved. I pulled him on to me and we fell free in the corridor as the resistance of the cot suddenly diminished and the gap left by the door shrank to a few inches.

We stood and watched the door compress the cot frame to its limit. 'Come on Fergy,' I said again, and we set off down the corridor, both of us panting in the rarified eighty-per-cent air.

I knew what I was looking for, but I didn't know where they kept them. I remembered somehow being brought here on a powered trolley and I meant to ride on one again – with me doing the steering.

Luck was with us. I heard the sound of a trolley coming towards us and I pulled Fergy with me to hide behind a stack of empty packing moulds.

As the sound grew nearer I judged the moment and then heaved. The moulds fell to the floor, forming a flimsy barrier. The man stopped his trolley and got off to examine the obstruction.

I stepped forward brandishing the cot leg and he stepped back to the wall and stayed there. I made Ferguson sit on the forward part of the truck and I got on the driving platform.

Turning the lever to the right made us go backwards. So I pushed it to the other side, and we moved forward, nosing aside the fallen moulds.

We drove along the corridor to an intersection, which led to the main hall. There was something I needed there.

Along one wall were rows of black plastic cylinders, some large, some small enough to be carried on a man's back. In one corner was a neat stack of breathing masks and tubes. I took a couple.

'Get yourself plugged in,' I said to Ferguson, tossing him a breathing mask.

I went over to the cylinders and picked out a small one, screwing in one end of the tube and placing the mask at the other end over my mouth and nose.

The guards used these things when they had to visit very low-oxygen environments. Placing my arms through the loops hanging from the cylinder I hoisted it on to my back as I had seen them do, and breathed deeply.

Delicious! The atmosphere from the bottle reinvigorated me. I had not realized how much I had been missing the atmosphere of the retribution cell.

Ferguson smiled at me from behind his mask. He was breathing full-strength atmosphere for maybe the first time ever. I hoped he felt as good as I did and then wondered just why I had got him to come along with me after the fracas in the cell.

He was a pleasant enough sort. We had often sat next to each other at nutrition time to swap sleep experiences. If I had a friend, it was he. But few of us had real friends. Only when we slept could we form relationships that were really satisfactory.

'Come on,' said Ferguson.

I jumped. I had for an instant almost forgotten where I was. For at that moment, thinking about Ferguson, I had realized that I should never see the girl on the fleeper again.

Not unless, after months or years of retribution I went back. . . .

'What now?' I asked. My voice sounded dull to me.

He looked at me, a little worried. 'How about eating?' he said.

Then I realized that I was starving. It was all this

oxygen. 'Right then,' I said, and we jumped on to the trolley, all gloom dispelled once more.

I steered the vehicle through the main gateway into the street. The guard didn't even look up as we went out.

Defying the Texecs was going to be easy!

As we cruised gently down the street I looked about me to see if I could spot any of the control cameras that must be trained on us. But they all appeared to be still.

Then we came to a corner window, and the screen inside was blank.

'I don't understand it,' I said. 'Before, when I was running along the streets they checked me everywhere I went.'

He snorted. 'They're scared now, you see,' he said. 'Before you were just some pathetic character running from a nightmare, and they made an example of you. We all watched you. Now there are two of us. We've defied the system – and got away with it so far. They daren't expose us, because we might encourage others. Not that they would get up to much in this atmosphere.'

'You're right,' I said, and took another whiff of oxygen.

There was more to Fergy than I thought. Perhaps there would be more to everybody than you thought – once you let them breathe properly.

Ahead was a Texec nutrition store. I had looked into the window of such places in dim curiosity before, never thinking that I could go in.

Not that I thought anything would happen to me if I went in. It was just one of the rules that you didn't, so you didn't.

We drew up and went in.

Looking back now, it seems hardly credible that our going into a Texec nutrition store should take so much resolve. But at the time it was an act of defiance that seemed to us the height of audacity. And, perhaps, it was indeed.

The little man behind the counter couldn't have thought we were Texecs, because we just didn't look or smell like

Texecs. They all had that sleek, well-groomed look that comes from habitually breathing good atmosphere – for at least twelve hours out of twenty-four – and living on first-class nutrition. We didn't have that look at all.

'What are you fellows going to have?'

That was the question he had been trained to ask everybody who came in. It was inconceivable that anyone but a Texec should come in so, despite our appearance, and despite our odour, he took us for granted.

'Nutrition,' I said.

'Yes, but what *kind*?' he asked.

I didn't know what to say. 'I think they can choose,' said Ferguson.

Choose? I had always accepted what had been put in front of me. I had never even dreamed of a place where they gave you a choice. Nutriment was nutriment and drink was drink. That was all there was to it.

'What shall we have?' I asked Fergy.

'Search me,' he said.

'What shall we have?' I asked the little fellow.

He seemed pleased. 'Well, the faunasim is better than usual today,' he said. 'I think the reprocessor has been overhauled.'

'OK,' I said. 'Faunasim it is.'

'And you too?'

Ferguson said yes, him too. Neither of us asked what faunasim was.

We stood there. The little man seemed flustered. 'Anything else?' he asked. We said no. 'Well, er, I'll be as quick as I can.'

'Thank you,' I said. This appeared to give him some relief.

'Well, er, excuse me,' he said, and bent below the counter.

Ferguson and I looked at each other in surmise. The little man straightened up. In his hands was a tray and on the tray were two loaded plates.

20

Our presence seemed to cause him embarrassment. 'Anything wrong?' I said.

'Oh, no . . . but where are you going to sit?' Again, Ferguson and I looked at each other and turned round to see the room behind us.

It was furnished with a number of tiny tables, none of which had more than six chairs round it. 'Over there, I suppose,' I said, waving an arm towards the middle of the room, hoping that that was where you were supposed to sit. 'And now could we have the food?'

Apparently offended, the little man came out from behind his counter carrying his tray and then, ignoring our outstretched hands walked right past us towards the tables.

For an instant we stood where we were. What was he up to? Why was he taking our food away? It was all too much. Taking a quick drag of oxygen, I went after him.

'Hey!' He did not turn round until he reached one of the tables. 'Will this do?' he asked. Do what? I shrugged.

Then he took the plates from the tray and put them on the table.

He made a gesture of invitation, said: 'Enjoy your meal, gentlemen,' and withdrew. Ferguson and I sat at the table at the places where the plates were laid, looked at each other, laughed, shrugged, and began to eat.

It was delicious. I had never known that nutriment could taste like this. In a state approaching ecstacy, I gobbled the food down.

Ferguson was the first one to ease up. He had eaten more recently than I.

'What made you ask for me?' he said.

'You were the first person I thought of,' I said. 'I'm sorry.'

'Sorry!' The protest was like a small explosion. 'I haven't had such fun awake in my life! Don't apologize, ever.'

He went on: 'Until today my wakeful existence was totally uneventful. Nothing had ever happened to me until I was picked up by these guards who told me you wanted me as a witness. I wasn't curious even then. I couldn't even remember who you were. But when they took me into that cell I could see something was happening. Suddenly I was interested.'

'The cell was oxygen rich,' I said.

'I see. Well, that explains it partly, but there was more to it than that. Hitting that guard, just like you do in dreams sometimes – I was astonished.

'For the first time in my wakeful I was watching something actually happen, watching somebody actually doing something. I found it, well, inspiring.'

'Good,' I said. 'With me, it was just the oxygen they gave me. It started me thinking for the first time. Bet they don't make that mistake a second time.'

We both laughed, and then stopped as we thought at the same time of the transgressors against the atmosphere rules who would follow me into the retribution cells.

'They'll have a rough time,' I said.

'But there's nothing we can do about it,' he said. I agreed.

'What we have to worry about now is us,' he said. 'We've broken out of the system, but it's still got to go on supporting us. We've got to go on consuming nutriment and atmosphere – more than our share, as we've got to look after ourselves – and we aren't going to offer anything in return. We'll throw the whole thing out of balance.'

There was much in what he said. For every being in Lemington there was a living space, a daily portion of nourishment and drink, an entitlement of vestments, a dream programme, a daily task. Each was entwined with or dependent upon the other. The task was generally meaningless, but the rule was austere and inflexible. Or so we had been taught, and so we believed.

It was all neatly balanced out, finely calculated upon a basis of reciprocation. Except for us.

We had just eaten another's allotment of food, we were breathing oxygen that the task of another had paid for. We were unbalancing the ledger of existence. How far would the repercussions of our nonconformity spread? It was an unanswerable question.

'One thing I'm certain of,' said Ferguson. 'And that is that the Texecs will regard us as an intolerable nuisance. They'll try either to get rid of us altogether or to work us back into the system so that it's balanced out again.'

'You're right,' I said. 'But I don't see what they can do.'

With our uncontrolled supply of stolen oxygen, we were more than a match for their guards – who were totally unused to coping with resistance.

I took a breath from the mask almost without thinking. It was becoming a habit. A good habit.

'They'll try and take us unawares, when we are asleep, or something like that,' I said. 'We'll have to be careful.'

'We needn't be too careful,' disagreed Ferguson. 'I mean, they don't even know where we are.'

'I'm sure you are wrong,' I said.

'You're right,' said a voice in my left ear.

I stood up, spun round, knocked over my chair, sent my plate clattering to the ground. Behind me, I could hear Ferguson getting to his feet.

The Texec in front of us stood head and shoulders above me, and even more above Ferguson. His face was strong and a brownish-cream in colour. His eyes, too, were strange in colour, the irises surrounded by a white that was almost pure.

His hair was thick, and grew to within two or three inches of his eyebrows. He smiled, and I saw that his teeth grew so close to one another that they touched.

'We do know where you are, you see,' he said.

His clothes hung easily upon him and he moved slightly inside them.

'Shall we sit down?' he said, picking up my chair with one hand and making a gesture towards it with the other.

'Er, yes.'

We sat, and immediately he lifted his hand above his head and clicked his finger and thumb together.

23

The little man from behind the counter was at his side in a flash.

'What were you eating?' the Texec asked me. 'Er, fer, um,' I said. 'Faunasim,' said the little man. 'I hope it will be all right. I didn't know, you see . . .'

The Texec interrupted him. 'Well, get some more then and clear this up,' he said.

He sounded just like I sounded to myself in dreamstate. That same firm voice. Those tones were delivered by one accustomed to giving orders.

I looked quickly at Ferguson. He sat there, hunched up, miserable-looking. His appearance reminded me of how he looked when he came into my cell earlier that day.

My backbone straightened itself. I lifted my head. I had no desire to look defeated like Ferguson.

'So you know where we are,' I said. 'What do you propose to do about it?'

'Nothing much,' said the Texec.

I was astonished. I had defied his seniors, run amok in their retribution block, eaten their food – and here they were, sending a representative to tell me that they planned to do nothing much about me.

The little man brought me a fresh plate of faunasim. Before serving me, he placed a glass of something before the Texec, who did not look up.

Which would show the more defiance – to eat the food, or to ignore it? I noticed that Ferguson had not touched his plate since the arrival of the Texec, so I decided to eat.

I took a mouthful before saying anything.

'There's not much you can do, is there?' I said.

'Oh, yes, a great deal,' said the Texec, leaning towards me. I sensed his strength and knew that he was speaking the truth. 'But we choose not to. We make rules and expect them to be kept – but when anyone chooses to defy them so blatantly, so determinedly as yourself, why, we reward them.'

'Reward them?' I knew it sounded foolish, but I could think of nothing else to say.

'Oh, yes. Anyone like you – and there are a few each year – who breaks out, shows courage, initiative, intelligence . . . well, we invite them to become one of us.'

'A Texec?'

He nodded. 'Yes. Up to a point, anyway. After all, we Texecs don't have a monopoly of talent. We are always on the look-out for new material. That's how we manage to run Lemington so successfully.'

'You must have a funny idea of success,' I said. Ferguson looked horrified, but I knew I was right. The more defiance from me, the more this Texec would take to me.

He laughed. 'I know just what you mean,' he said. 'Just a few people – we Texecs – enjoying perpetual wakeful privilege in the form of high atmosphere allowances, unlimited quantities of nutrition, a liberal statutory sleep requirement, when the bulk of the world is half-starved, semi-suffocated, unconscious for two-thirds of the time?' I nodded.

He went on: 'Well look at it this way. Somebody has to run the world. To do this they *need* the oxygen, *need* the nutrition. And they're too busy to dream. Think of that!'

I thought of that. And I was reminded again that by breaking out I could have lost her for ever. Never again would I visit our island or travel on a fleeper, pick the succulents and wash in the lake.

Ferguson didn't help. Obviously his thoughts were on similar lines to mine, and he began to weep. I was tempted in an instant of desperate weakness to do likewise.

But just in time the Texec pushed back his chair, signalling to me to do the same. He walked towards the door and as he passed the counter spoke to the little man, who smiled and nodded his head and scribbled on a pad.

We walked out into the street, leaving Ferguson with his head buried in his arms, his shoulders heaving.

The young man took a small device from his pocket and clapped it over his nose and mouth, breathing deeply once or twice. I envied him this miniature inhaler. My plastic

25

cylinder, so recently a treasured piece of booty, now seemed big and clumsy.

Behind us, Ferguson's wailing grew, curling out of the café door like a tentacle of misery, gripping me by the throat.

I felt concern but knew that it would be fatal for me to show it. The Texec volunteered an answer to my unspoken question. 'They'll make him repay the oxygen and nutrition, of course, but he'll be back on dreamstate within three months. We needn't worry about him.'

Poor Ferguson! He had taken a taste of freedom and it had been too strong. Now he faced three months of living death and then, a half-life for the rest of his existence. Hastily I took a breath from the mask.

'Before we resume our conversation,' said the young man, 'I must tell you my name. It is Antonio.'

'And mine. . .' I said.

'Don't bother,' he said.

We were walking down a street that I had never seen before. It was brighter than most, and the sky had been freshly painted. It was more populated, too, and once or twice I had to pause or step aside to let others pass.

'So the majority of people are obliged to live a diminished and undemanding existence,' he was saying, 'so that their nutritive and respiratory requirements are kept to a minimum. In compensation for this their sleepstate is enhanced by vivid and pleasurable dreams.'

We turned into a narrow alleyway, brightly lit.

I heard his quick indrawing of breath, his lungs grabbing every cubic centimetre of atmosphere they could. The sudden grip on my arm was painful.

White-faced and rigid, he pointed with a trembling finger. 'LOOK,' he said. 'GARBAGE.'

True enough, in the middle of the walkway, still steaming gently, was a discarded plate of nutriment, half consumed.

For an instant he stood there, motionless. Then he released my arm, darted forward, picked up the plate, checked the number and ran to the waste distributor a few yards along the walkway.

He came back to me, looking worried. 'Just don't tell anyone what you've seen, that's all,' he said.

I wasn't going to. All of us, Sleepees and Texecs alike, were trained to dispose of waste the instant it was created. Failure to do so was usually regarded as the result of mind-sickness and was treated accordingly.

It was shocking indeed to find an unconsumed plate of A-quality nutriment lying in the walkway of a Texec precinct – so shocking that it was best to forget the whole thing.

We walked together for a short way more, saying nothing, when Antonio took a key from his pocket, waved it at a door and stepped inside, beckoning me with his head to follow.

He was panting. My own breath came in great gasps. Our walk, coupled with the emotion of seeing that garbage, had exhausted me.

I lifted my inhaler to my face.

'Don't bother,' he said. 'Won't be long now.'

We were standing in a tiny sealed lobby. A concealed atmosphere exchanger hissed. I went a little dizzy. The atmosphere of the airlock had come up to the standard of the apartment's interior, and the inner door swung open.

He was waiting for us.

'Here at last!' said my chief interrogator, smiling cordially.

3

He came towards me, hand extended. There was no doubt-
ng the warmth of his welcome.

'Ah, Phillips,' he said. 'We meet in the flesh, and in
appier circumstances.' He took my hand and looked down
t me. He was taller than I had imagined, but his colour
as as poor as it had appeared to be on the screen.

'My name isn't Phillips,' I said.

'It is now,' he replied and, putting a bony hand on
y cringing shoulder, steered me towards a great and
rilliantly-lit room beyond an archway at the end of the
ntrance hall.

'You see,' he said, as we walked slowly along, 'I took a
ancy to you the first time you appeared on the interro-
ation screen. "There's a fellow with his wits about him," I
aid to myself, "despite his being a Sleepee".'

I looked at him and frowned. 'I don't understand,' I said.

Here the other Texec intervened.

'They don't use the term Sleepee among themselves,' he
aid. 'They just think of themselves as ordinary individ-
als.'

'Just so,' said the interrogator. And then, to me: 'You've
lot to learn.'

I stopped. His hand slipped from my shoulder. 'I don't
nderstand,' I said again.

'I smash your screen, break out of your retribution block,
it your guard, steal oxygen and a trolley, take a meal in a
exec café, break all the rules, and now . . . you say you
ook a fancy to me. If I'd known you approved of me, I
ouldn't have done all those things. . . . But you threatened
e with ultimate punishment. And now I've gone even

more wrong you're treating me like a favourite pupil. Just what are you trying to do?'

As I spoke I became frightened. It was as though my words were of their own volition expressing a disquiet of the inner self, one which I had refused consciously to acknowledge. I looked around quickly, in search of any possible escape.

His hand was back on my shoulder. There was a lot of strength in his fingers. I knew I hadn't a chance, even if I needed one.

'You see,' he said, 'Lemington needs individuals like you. You may think that the administration is best left to us Texecs, but the problems sometimes grow too much for those born to deal with them. So from time to time we bring in new blood – as and when it makes itself known to us.'

'And I did?'

He nodded.

'By breaking out of dormy, taking all that oxygen . . . defying the Texecs?'

He nodded again. 'You showed spirit,' he said. 'And a certain amount of ingenuity.'

I started to tell him that anyone would have done the same in my circumstances – a foul-up in the dreamstate, extra oxygen while in an excited condition . . . anyone.

Except poor old Ferguson. And one or two others.

He stopped me.

'You have a lot to learn,' he said again. 'But when you have learned what we have to teach you, you will have a considerable role to play in the running of Lemington.'

Then he turned and walked out slowly. The other Texec went with him.

They left me alone in that lofty, brilliant chamber. I looked at the ceiling curving upwards to the summit, with its bright, white surface decorated and picked out here and there with gold.

On the walls hung pictures in dully-shining frames of Texecs in rich dress. Here and there they had hung material of glowing reds and purples which fell in folds to the floor, itself composed of rich yellow substance, covered in places with rectangular and oval pieces of stuff in colours of a depth and vibrancy I had never encountered in a wakeful state.

And such light! It hurt my eyes, but I could not close them as I took in my surroundings.

'Am I in dreamstate?' I wondered to myself. I must have uttered my thoughts, for the young man who had returned without my hearing him, replied.

'You're as awake as I am,' he said. 'Now, sit down.'

I looked around me, could see no benches or chairs, so lowered myself to the floor.

The young man burst out laughing, and held out his hand. I gave him mine, and he pulled me to my feet again.

'Not there, *there!*' he said, jabbing a finger at a strange arrangement of rectangular boxes covered with a golden cloth.

I approached the object, poked it, prodded it, confirmed its solidity, turned my back on it, squatted towards it, putting my hands behind me and to each side of me to cushion any fall.

'Perfect!' he said, throwing himself into one of the objects. Seeing him do this, I allowed myself to fall backwards into mine.

It was an extraordinary feeling. The chair – for chair it was – seemed to envelop me in comfort. Pliant to my slightest movement, receptive to the smallest irregularity in my skinny frame, it offered support wherever I touched it, caressing me, urging me to sink back and relax.

I was seated, yet nowhere did my bones seek a way out of their confines when they took my weight. I thought of my vertebrae trying to saw their way out of my back as I lay awake on a dormitory plank; I thought of my top thigh sockets trying to press their way out of my buttocks as I sat for ages outside the stumber dispensary, and I marvelled.

'Such comfort,' I said. 'I never knew it existed. What is this thing?'

'It's an easy chair,' said the young man. 'Stuffed with hair.'

He smiled and bounced up and down, encouraging me by signs to do the same.

I smiled back and bounced too, but I couldn't help wondering about whose hair it had been.

4

THE following weeks were spent in an uneasy luxury. I breathed the Texecs' air, ate their nutriment, shared their homes and their company.

I was taken through their mysteries and introduced to their way of life. They were, I learned, dedicated to their ideal: they were not a race apart from the Sleepees but a class apart. They were necessary to maintain the habitat. Without them, Lemington would collapse. If all the Texecs became Sleepees, there would be no one to supervise the maintenance of the air conditioners or nutriment reprocessors, no one to oversee the administration of stumber distribution, the allocation of sleeping quarters, or to see that discipline was maintained.

If, on the other hand, all the Sleepees were to become Texecs, with their high oxygen and nutriment requirements, then there would simply not be enough of these necessities to go round; the balance of artificiality would be destroyed and the race would perish.

But as things were existence hung in a fine balance, and if it did not thrive, it at least continued.

The Texecs made much of their sacrifices to duty. Often they would sigh with envy at the thought of having an obligatory sixteen hours sleep a day, with a rich and incessant supply of dreams being pumped in.

When they spoke like that, I would challenge them.

'You make the dreams yourselves,' I said. 'You know what they're like. Why not feed a few to yourselves?'

They shrugged, and waved their hands, and said it was not the same. You couldn't enjoy a dream you had made yourself, could you now?

I shrugged and smiled, and forbore to say that they could take a dream feed-in from another Texec if they wanted something with a surprise ending.

And I also did not say that their wakeful condition was in many ways more pleasant than many a Sleepee's dream-state.

Don't ask me how I learned the wisdom of keeping my mouth shut. I just knew it without being told, that's all.

Anyway, I couldn't tell them how paltry dreamstate was when I was aching for it all the time. Often I would have to bite my lips and dig my nails into my palms to stop myself from screaming out for a stumber pill and a headline to the dreamstate.

I would risk the fear, I would defy the teeth in the sky, I would face madness for the sake of seeing her and the lake, the valley and the island again.

Sometimes I felt that I would go mad anyway for the lack of a sight of her. The feelings were worst at night. Time and time again I would wake bathed in sweat as I yearned for a return to the lake and the island, for the feel of a fleeper, the taste of a succulent and the touch of her.

I was sure that my Texec masters knew about my cravings, and approved of my resistance to them. They thought, I suppose, that I was trying as hard as I could to become one of them – and that forswearing the Sleepee drug was part of my endeavour.

And perhaps they were right. Now I don't know exactly what I felt. But I knew somehow that my self-denial was tempering my spirit and giving me courage. I knew that one day I would need to excel in matters of courage.

32

I had no idea then of the circumstances that would test me; but I knew they would come.

It could have been my persisting sense of alienation that prevented me and my Texec acquaintances from establishing any form of intimacy. Although I was treated with cordiality, to which I dutifully responded, they never talked to me as they did to each other. Even when they argued among themselves there was between them an exclusive rapport which I was unable to analyse.

The only Texec with whom I was able to establish anything like even the impersonal camaraderie I had found with my fellow-Sleepees in the dormys or on the benches of the stumber dispensaries was Marie, my principal tutor.

She was a great, tall woman with a rich skin, black eyes, and a brilliant smile which came readily. Of all my teachers she was the most interesting, spending most of her time with me in explaining the complex system of mechanical-biological balances employed to keep our civilization alive.

The lessons were frightening. They taught me the precariousness of existence, and I learned to value my life less.

The teaching sessions with Marie lasted for an hour or perhaps two every day. She talked to me, gave me files to read (which I found difficult) and gave me essays to write (which I found easy, although I had to be careful about which ideas I put down).

The facts she gave to me one day she would test me on the next. She turned it into a sort of game, and under her tuition I found that the process of learning became easier all the time.

I was astonished, too, at how rapidly I acquired a facility for fluent reading and writing. The Sleepees were not issued with a great abundance of reading material, and implements for writing were hard to come by – an injustice which caused little unrest, for few Sleepees could see the purpose of literacy, and most were too idle to pursue it.

As a result, a great number of Sleepees had forgotten

those rudiments of scholarship which in one way or another they had once acquired.

I, as in other ways, was an exception, but I found nevertheless that most of the Texecs were far more proficient in these matters than I.

So that was another skill of theirs that I was determined to gain for myself.

They liked me for it.

During our long conversations together, Marie and I would sometimes wander about the Texec compound, a communal open square with a lofty, well-lit sky, and with a generous atmosphere supply.

It was at the centre of the Texec's living quarter complex and from it ran a number of alleyways so that a Texec could make his way from his own residence to that of a colleague without going outside.

The provision of the square and the alleyways – all staunchly sealed against the weaker atmosphere of the outside, of course – meant that a Texec's house had to have its hermetic door only where it opened to the exterior.

Thus the Texecs were able to open and close their interior doors simply by turning a handle: they used doors simply to preserve and establish privacy and not to keep different grades of atmosphere from merging.

This was one of the many things to which I found it difficult to become accustomed.

But nothing excited or mystified me more than what I later came to call the House of the Little People.

It happened one morning shortly after the illumination had come to full brightness. Marie and I were strolling through the square discussing the theories of sewage reprocessing chemistry, as I remember, when I first heard those strange voices.

They had an extraordinary shrillness, and were raised as though in great passion. Marie, incredibly, appeared not to hear. In fact her questioning of my knowledge grew more pressing. I tried to answer her questions but found myself too distracted by these voices to pay her much attention.

She was beginning to get angry with me when the door of this house opened, and a minute figure, almost perfect in its proportions, came running out.

I assumed that it was female, for its hair and skin were extremely fine. It moved with a tolerable degree of articulation, and its limbs worked with great rapidity.

But they were too small to generate sufficient speed to outpace the female Texec of normal size who gave it chase. The moment of drama was brief: the big Texec overtook the little being within a few paces and overpowered it simply by grabbing its arm.

The midget went red-faced and screamed shrilly and struggled desperately, but to no avail. Inexorably the full-sized female retraced their steps to the house, went in, and slammed the door.

There was the sound of a blow, as delivered by the open hand, a wailing, a voice raised in anger, and a silence.

'Come on, Phillips,' said Marie.

'But – didn't you see – that minute creature! What could it have been? It was smaller than the smallest Sleepee I've ever seen. Marie! You saw! Tell me what it was?'

Marie laughed. 'Stop babbling! No, I didn't see it. And neither did you.'

'I did! Anyway, you must have heard it.'

'No, I did not. And neither did you, Phillips. Remember that. You didn't see it. You didn't hear it. Now. Once again . . . describe to me the functions of a formalyn sluice.'

I swallowed hard and tried to reply.

Maybe Marie hadn't heard or seen what I had. But it was difficult to believe her. And if I couldn't trust Marie, whom could I trust?

During the following week I noticed, or thought I noticed, that Marie tried to avoid the square during our walks, preferring the tennis courts, or the swimming pool, or even some of the nearby dormy streets outside.

But I worked against her, hoping that she would not

notice, and once or twice I contrived to make it impossible to avoid the square.

When we went past the house of the little people, I pretended unconcern. I was less interested in the house than in the way Marie would observe me as we walked past it.

I felt pleased, convincing myself that I had betrayed less than she had – pleased, but not entirely confident.

One evening as the external lights, in obedience to their programme, were dimmed to a more restful intensity and the internal lights within the Texecs' apartments were turned up, I walked from my apartment to the square.

I made my way towards the house of the little people, glancing about me as I did so to ensure that no one was observing me. There was only an old man, sitting with his back to me in the far corner of the square.

When I got there I ensured once more that I was not over-looked, and peered through the windows.

Only one gave me any clue to the interior, the rest being either shuttered or of a one-way transparency. What I could see through that one window increased rather than satisfied my curiosity.

In the gloom I could see a quantity of small chairs and tables and in the corner there was a basin and a tap set a good foot closer to the floor than was the custom. Lined up against the wall opposite the window was a collection of peculiar items, which I was unable to recognise with the exception of a few miniature representations of the human form, dressed in odd-looking clothes, and a scaled-down version of an electric trolley.

Overwhelmed by a desire to discover more I made my way to the door, and with a recklessness that I would normally have considered insane, pushed it open and walked in.

I walked into a fist in the face.

Staggering back from the blow I suddenly choked as someone behind me put the crook of his elbow round my throat and clapped a cloth impregnated with some volatile substance over my nose and mouth.

It felt for a moment as though someone were pumping my lungs full of air, fresh and terribly cold. Then I realized that the expansion of my lungs was due to an alarmed diaphragm desperately working so that they could inhale when there was nothing to inhale.

Then I felt as though I had somehow become enveloped in my own lungs, which had become inflated to the size of a small room.

A choir of ten thousand sang in each ear and my head rocked on its foundations before everything went red, then black, and then I sank into a pit which had no bottom.

I came to in my own room. How I had got there I did not know or care. My head ached and my tongue seemed to have grown hair. I staggered over to the basin, drank, was sick, felt better, returned to bed and slept, only to be pursued by midget Texecs with giant fists. I ran from them and although I never saw them, I knew always that they were on my heels.

The next day I resolved never again to go exploring on my own. Nobody said anything to me, but they knew – I could tell by the way they treated me. Not a word, not a glance was out of place. Their behaviour was too perfect, and that's how I knew that they all knew.

I was unable to dismiss the midgets from my mind until one morning, Antonio came to my room and shook me awake.

'Come on,' he said. 'Quickly.'

I tumbled out of bed and started pulling on some clothes when he said: 'You can do that on our way. Grab your clothes and follow me. Come on, now.'

Keeping up with Antonio with my pants half on and a bundle of clothes in my arms was not easy, but somehow I made it to the trolley.

'Hang on,' he said, and drove off, causing me to lose my balance and sit heavily on the platform.

The usual number of Sleepees were mooning about in indeterminate wakestate. They stared at me incuriously as, moving along the road at about five times walking pace, I heaved my pants over my buttocks and did up the belt, removed the top half of my Texec sleepsuit and pulled on my shirt. I saw an old man, seated, looking at me. Then we turned a corner and I could see him no more.

'Where are we going?' I shouted to Antonio.

'Y-six.'

'Y-six? What for?'

'They've a little trouble down there. You'll see.'

We could hear the trouble before we got to it. A regular thud could be heard above the sibilant noise of our travel, and as we drew closer to the sound, we could hear voices raised in excitement.

Antonio stopped the machine at the end of an alleyway leading off the trunk thoroughfare.

It was an ordinary kind of dormy street, low-skied, dim, with a cement wall running down each side relieved by a series of hermetic doors at intervals of some fifteen feet.

Antonio jumped off the trolley and went up to a Texec I had not seen before.

'Are we too late?'

'Nope. They're still going strong. Don't know how they do it. You can see them in there.'

He pointed to a service centre door on the alleyway corner.

'Right,' said Antonio. 'Coming?' I went after him.

'Hey *you*. You a Sleepee?' It was the Texec. Antonio replied for me. 'He's a protégé. He's with me. He's OK.'

The Texec shrugged.

'Who's he?' I asked.

'That's Snagl, head of security.' Antonio pushed open the swing doors into the centre.

'Security? I've never heard of that.'

'It was security picked you up when you went berserk,' said Antonio. 'Ah, there they are.'

On the screen before us was an image, all in red, of a dormy gone mad. Some of the occupants were blindly fighting among themselves; others were groping around for sanctuary, withdrawing rapidly every time they touched one another; some were cowering under the sleeping boards; others were attempting to dismantle the planks with their hands. Four of them – males – were acting in concert, using a sleeping plank as a battering ram against the hermetic.

The dimness of the image did not disguise that their expressions were uniformly of those crazed with terror or rage, or a mixture of the two.

'It's quite black in there,' said Antonio. 'I know,' I said. 'They are doing rather well in the dark, don't you think?' he asked. 'After all, they're pretty well dosed up with stumber.'

'Your own adrenalin can overcome it if you produce enough,' I said. 'After all, look what happened to me.'

'Yes, but there's a low degree of control over the nervous system.'

'Those four don't look as though they are doing too badly.'

We looked at the four Sleepee males still trying to batter down the door, which had been barred from the outside. Oblivious of our scrutiny through the infrared image apparatus, time after time they hurled themselves and their ram against the unyielding hermetic.

'How come I wasn't locked in when it happened to me?' I asked.

'You were too quick, I expect. They usually give us a good half-hour's warning.'

'Usually?'

'Well,' Antonio corrected himself. 'It doesn't happen all that often. But sometimes the wrong dream schedule gets into the impulsers, or an interruption in power supply causes chaos in the audio-sensory circuits. Whatever it is, the whole dormy usually screams together, and this gets picked up; and Security comes along, and shuts 'em in. They get over it quickly enough.'

'The Sleepees in there don't seem to be getting over it.'

'They soon will. They'll run out of atmosphere pretty soon.'

I nodded. There was enough atmosphere in a sealed dormy to support the catatonic Sleepees until they were ready to resume wakestate. But if they were to wake, let alone to move around as they were in there, then the oxygen would pretty soon run out.

'So they'll keel over?'

Antonio nodded.

'What then?'

Antonio shrugged. 'Most recover. After all, what's a touch of asphyxia to a Sleepee?'

What indeed? Already I was feeling discomfort in the rarefied atmosphere of outside. I wondered how I would feel inside the dormy.

I walked away from the screen and sat down. I did not want Antonio to suspect my feelings.

Just then the security man came in. He ignored me. Antonio spoke to him. 'Dreamfault?'

The security man nodded. 'Yep. A kinky tape did it. Annoying. It happens too often. The dream-makers should be more careful.'

I pretended not to hear, because I know I was hearing something forbidden. I had thought that every Texec was a dream-maker. He was a Texec because he made dreams. He made dreams because he was a Texec.

So there was yet another class. . . . I studied the security man closely.

He was absorbed with what was happening on the screen, and did not notice my study.

'There they go,' he said.

I got up to see. The occupants of the dormy were exhibiting signs now of acute oxygen starvation. Blind and weak, one by one they toppled. Within a short time, with the exception of their heaving rib cages, they were still.

The security man looked at the chronorecorder above the screen. 'Six hours,' he said. 'Then we'll open up.'

'Six hours?' I repeated. 'You're going to leave them in there for six hours?'

He looked at me. 'Well, they've only been in there ten,' he said.

'But they'll die,' I said.

'Not all of them,' said Antonio. 'Anyway, you can't frustrate the system.'

Marie helped a lot after that day, which was the day I learned there was more to worry about than the existence of forbidden midgets. She seemed to understand my feelings about those Sleepees, though we never talked about them. In addition to the regular lessons, she taught me games that built muscle, developed the eye and promoted articulation.

I always thought of her as being bigger, stronger, quicker than myself but suddenly, after a game of tens, she seemed much smaller. Smaller, even, than I.

She laughed as we flopped on the seat beside the court.

'You're getting better, Phillips,' she said. 'You'll be beating me soon.'

I felt pleased, too pleased. I looked down at the racket. 'It was the racket,' I said. 'It was the heavier racket. That was what helped.'

Again she laughed. 'That's not the point, you great softie,' she said. 'The difference is you. When you first came to me you were too weak to be able even to lift that racket. You had to use a special small model. But now . . . it's you. You're growing. You really are. Stand up.'

I stood up, and so did she. 'Look at me,' she said. I looked down into her face. 'Notice anything?' I shook my head.

'Really, Phillips,' she said. 'Sometimes I wonder why they took you on. You're so stupid sometimes! Don't you remember when we first met, you had to look up at me. Now you're looking down. I haven't shrunk, you know.'

I looked again. What she said was true. In the few weeks on full-strength atmosphere and on Texec nutriment, I had actually grown.

'You're getting to be a big man, now,' she said softly, and I looked at her and felt suddenly that I could pick her up

41

and run carrying her in my arms. I felt the energy inside me. I touched her hair. She pulled her head away.

'Come on,' she said. 'Let's take a shower.'

As we walked along to the shower rooms she took me through the global statistics on which the rules of the Lemington City were based.

'Sleepee population of the habitat?'

'Two million.'

'Texec population?'

'Three thousand.'

'Ideal Texec/Sleepee ratio?'

'One to five hundred on present habitat capacity, whatever that means. But . . .'

'Sleepee increase rate?'

'Minus three in two hundred. But . . .'

'Texec increase rate?'

'One in twenty. But how . . .'

'Target date for ideal ratio?'

'Well, that's one I've been trying to figure out, Marie. Assuming that the Texecs continue to increase their increase at present rates, and the Sleepees continue to increase their decrease rate at present rates, then it should be within the decade . . .'

She gave a strange, bitter laugh. 'No,' she said. 'That's not right. No one knows, although the answer I'm supposed to teach you is fifty years. If anyone asks you just say "fifty years" and shut up. Sounds crazy, but that's the way it is.'

'How come?'

We had reached the showers. Marie stopped and faced me. 'Well, that's really changing the subject,' she said. 'It's not really within my province, that one.'

'Do *you* know?'

'Yes, I know.'

'Then tell me.'

'No, Phillips, really. I mustn't. I've already said too much. Just forget it.'

She turned away. 'I'm taking a shower,' she said, and

42

pushed open the door. I followed her. 'Well tell me while you're in the shower. I'll take one with you.'

'No!' She shoved me. I pushed back. For an instant we struggled on the slippery tiles of the shower room. I felt my arms go round her.

'Please,' she said, quietly. Her hands pushed gently on my chest.

'Sorry,' I said, without knowing why, and went outside. I heard her push the bolt to and then I thought I could hear her sob. But within a minute the water was running and she sang.

I was still shaking when I went into my shower.

5

NEXT day, something had changed between the Texecs and me. I first noticed it when I went into the council chamber to observe a meeting of the stumber distribution co-ordinating committee.

My old inquisitor, Dmitri, was chairman and Antonio was also a member.

They were all talking when, late, I entered the chamber. Almost, but not quite imperceptibly, the chatter diminished as they noticed me, and then it rose again louder and more strident than before as though the ten or so people talking in that room had all decided to change the subject under discussion.

I went up to Dmitri and apologized for my unpunctuality – although in reality I had been made late because I had been on an errand for him.

'Late?' he cried. 'Why my boy, of course you're late. Think nothing of it, we don't.' And unaccountably he went into a fit of laughter so boisterous that he had to be led to

43

a chair. One by one, the rest of the room joined in. I stood there bewildered, enveloped by the gales of laughter which swept about me.

Hands took mine, slapped me on the back, gripped me by the forearm. Eyes regarded mine, and heads shook themselves in a comradely yet sly way. Words were uttered which I could not hear, or could not understand, and fresh bellows of laughter added regularly to the noise.

It was as though I had uttered some supreme witticism, although I could see no particular merit in my formal words of apology.

Eventually, however, I gave way and joined in.

'Ha-ha-ha,' I cried. 'Ho-ho-ho.'

And then, as suddenly as it had started, it stopped. And I was left there laughing hysterically at a joke I had not seen, in an otherwise silent room.

Dmitri had seated himself at the head of the long committee table. Banging his gavel he called the meeting to order, saying: 'To business, gentlemen, to business.'

He did not look well. Laughter makes heavy demands upon a man's lung capacity, and Dmitri's lungs had been subjected to sporadic overwork for many years. Mine had always been overworked until now. But I was younger.

I took a chair by the wall, but Dmitri beckoned me to the table.

'Come and sit here with the committee. After all, you're practically one of us now,' he said, and grinned down the table.

It was all very strange, but I did my best to look unconcerned as, murmuring thanks, I pulled up a chair.

'Item one,' he said. 'To discuss accommodation at precinct stumber distribution point forty-two. Texecs on supervision duty there have found it excessively noisy and uncomfortable – and inefficient – to the point that their hours of discomfort have been extended beyond tolerable limits.'

'Not to mention the Sleepees,' said a voice.

'Quite so. Not to mention the Sleepees,' said Dmitri.

44

'No. I'm making a serious point,' said the voice which belonged to a grey-haired Texec who had a habit of sighing deeply about twice a minute. 'Some of them had to wait so long for their pills that they missed out on a dosage. If that happened more than once or twice, it could be serious.'

'You mean they might start feeling rebellious again?' The speaker was a young Texec renowned for his stupidity – he had run the risk more than once of a downgrading to Sleepee status, I had heard.

'No, no, you dope . . .'

Dmitri interrupted them. 'We are not here to discuss the effects of stumber withdrawal – although if we were, Phillips here could no doubt tell us a lot,' and he nodded a smile in my direction. 'Nevertheless . . .' He paused.

Then he beckoned to me. 'Phillips, would you mind?' To the others: 'Excuse me, gentlemen.'

I pushed back my chair and went to the head of the table. 'Come here,' he said quietly. 'Look, would you just go and take the intake pressure reading at forty-five conditioner plant. I'm not sure the figures we're getting are too reliable just now.'

Then he said: 'Sorry about the meeting. But it's one of our dullest. Come and have dinner tomorrow instead.'

'Thank you,' I said, and walked out. I closed the door after me. But instead of leaving immediately I leaned against the lintel, my ear not too far from the crack.

I could not hear Dmitri's words, but he sounded angry – and he did not sound like a man who was addressing a meeting he considered dull.

I was troubled on the way to the conditioner intake. But at least I had no bother finding the way. I had just come from there on my way to the committee room, and the reading was exactly the same as it had been when I had taken it an hour earlier.

The apparatus was working perfectly, as I knew it would be.

But what happened the following evening and the next day

threw me into an ecstacy of confusion. When I called at Marie's for tuition in the morning I was greeted, not by her, but by a Texec who told me that his name was Helgon.

It was a strange name, but he had a strange way of speaking and it sounded natural when he spoke it.

'I'm your new . . . tutor,' he said. 'I've been asked to tell you about the different habitats.'

Different habitats? Surely Lemington had just the one habitat?

I must have looked puzzled, for he continued: 'Lemington is only one of many habitats, you know. This is common knowledge among the Texecs but the Sleepees, of course, concentrate their minds inwardly.' He smiled crookedly and shrugged as though indicating that he did not wish to give offence. I didn't offend easily.

'That's all right,' I said. 'I didn't know. I'd never thought about it. Go on . . .'

'Well, we understand each other then. I'd been told you probably didn't know . . . As I was saying, there are many habitats similar to this. It is generally believed that they are all contained within a great globe, and are connected by tubes which burrow through that globe. There are other theories. Among the more popular: that we are placed within a disc, rather than a globe; or that each habitat is itself a separate globe, or disc, and that together the habitats comprise a conglomerate system which is suspended in an enormous void and is held together by the tubes which incidentally provide the connections.'

I had been standing. Suddenly I felt as though I had to sit.

Helgon laughed sympathetically.

'It must come as something of a shock the first time,' he said. 'It is difficult for me to appreciate, as it is something I have always known about, but I can sympathize.'

He continued: 'I prefer the first of the theories: it is so much neater – but I must confess that the others have yet to be disproved.'

46

'Surely the best way to disprove them – if what you tell me is true – is to prove the first theory,' I said.

'Indeed. But it is not easy. The first theory has been commonly held for as long as anyone can remember. It did not have to be proved. It was simply accepted. It requires proof now only because of the existence of new and less satisfactory theories. But we digress,' he said.

'The reason for it not being common knowledge among the Sleepees that there are habitats other than their own is the decline of communication between them.'

'Between the habitats or between the Sleepees?' I asked.

Again he laughed. 'Well, both I suppose, but I really meant between the habitats,' he said. 'As you know the relationship between consumer demand and consumables, between waste and reprocessor in Lemington is very finely judged.'

I nodded.

'Well, it's the same for all habitats. None of them have much capacity to spare – so none of them welcomes visitors. And indeed, the absence of a consumer can cause as much upheaval as the presence of an extra one, so they don't like people leaving, either. Therefore . . .'

'Declining communications,' I finished for him.

'Just so. Which is a shame, considering what resources are available for transportation between habitats.'

'Through the tubes?'

'Through the tubes, yes. That's how I got here last night.'

'You *got* here, from another habitat? How come, if it's so difficult to leave – or to arrive?'

Helgon shrugged. 'Well, Cubale – where I come from – wanted me to go. Just why they wanted me to go I'm not prepared to discuss. But Lemington wanted me to come. So here I am.'

His expression was strange, defensive.

'Why should Lemington want you to come?'

'Maybe they want someone to go. How should I know? Anyway, let's get on with the job in hand. They told me to tell you about the other habitats, so I suppose I'd better.'

47

He talked about strange places with odd names and described their ways of living, and how their inhabitants differed in custom, and sometimes language and appearance too, from those of Lemington. One of them was called Blasintium. It was a name I would have cause to remember well.

It was all very interesting and I was sorry later that I had not paid better attention, but I was feeling very worried for myself.

Helgon was already there later in the day when I went to Dmitri's for dinner. I was surprised to see him there when I arrived, for I had deliberately come early to give myself a chance to talk to Dmitri.

Dmitri, though, was not in a mood to be talked to. As I entered his drawing room he saw me immediately and, looking into my eyes all the time, came slowly across to me.

My smile of greeting felt like a permanent fixture. I tried to think of something to say but the words in my head all sounded impertinent. So I didn't speak.

'Ah, Phillips, my favourite Sleepee,' he said, putting an arm round my shoulder. 'Helgon has been telling me all about how fascinated you are by the idea of other regions.'

Again I was at a loss for words. No doubt in my anxiety to make a favourable impression with Helgon – as I was with everybody – I had deceived him into thinking that I had been concentrating wholly upon his words.

The dinner was a strange affair. Dmitri and Helgon kept on bringing up the subject of inter-region travel. And Dmitri forced several of my fellow guests to relate their experiences. They were all highly enthusiastic about the pleasures of foreign travel, and all bemoaned the restrictions upon it.

I looked from one to the other in amazement. Never before had I heard the subject discussed. The Texecs were always too concerned with what was happening in their own precinct to bother overmuch about somebody else's.

And as for leisure travel, which they all kept talking

about with such enthusiasm – I had never heard such non-sense. The Texecs pursued pleasure in their own homes. And if their own homes proved inadequate in this respect – why, they simply improved them.

But as usual, I went along with the Texecs, being as affable as I could, showing no signs of my suspicions. I knew that if I stepped out of line just once, they would relegate me to the Sleepee ranks if they could – and if they couldn't, they would send me to some other place that was far worse than a Sleepee dream galley.

I looked round the assembly. 'Where's Marie?' I asked.

'She couldn't come, Phillips dear,' said old Gerda, whom they said lived with Dmitri. 'Would you care for a little more Pappel? It's been in dryfreeze for seventy-five years, so I know it's good.'

'Thanks, no. Why couldn't she come?'

'How about that, Phillips,' Antonio shouted from the other end of the table.

'What's that?' I smiled at Antonio, knowing that I was being sidetracked.

'Helgon here. He says he can fix a trip to Cubale for you. I don't know how, but if he says he can fix it, he can fix it.'

I know how, I thought. And so do you. I smiled.

Antonio, sensing perhaps that I knew he was trying to deceive me, went on, babbling a little. 'You lucky fellow, Phillips. You don't know how lucky you are. I've always longed to go up there . . .'

'*Down* there, you mean,' said Helgon, grinning, coming to the rescue.

'*Along* there,' said Dmitri, his voice crackling with ancient mirth.

Soon they all joined in. '*Over* there.' 'No, *in* there . . .' 'Not *in* there – *back* there!'

One of the guests, an old man sitting in the shadowy end of the room, kept quiet and still. The rest joined in the fun.

'Cubale – great!' 'Lucky fellow!' 'Wish I could come too . . .' 'Can't get away!'

I continued to smile.

49

'When?' I asked.

'That's the spirit,' said Antonio. 'What's wrong with now?'

'But have you had enough to eat?' asked old Gerda.

'I haven't had anything to eat,' I said.

'Fine, come on then,' said Antonio, and he and Helgon each took an arm and steered me out.

'Goodbye,' I shouted, but the door was shut behind me. They wouldn't have heard anyway. They were laughing too loudly.

Outside there was a trolley waiting. Helgon jumped on to the driver's platform. 'Get on then,' he said. I sat on the passenger section, moving over so that Antonio could take his place beside me.

We were moving off and the space beside me was still empty. I looked round and saw Antonio there. He waved. 'Er . . . say goodbye to Marie for me,' I shouted as we gathered speed.

He shouted something. It might have been 'Sure thing'. Or it might have been something else.

I held tight on to the handrail of the vehicle, which was going faster than regulations permitted.

Then as we were leaving the Texec compound for the main thoroughfare I caught sight of Marie. I would have jumped off, but we were going too fast. Then I was glad I had not been able to, for she was obviously embarrassed. She caught sight of me, half raised her hand to wave, changed her mind, dropped it to her side, turned her head away and began earnestly to study the object in front of her, which was a blank wall.

I had no wish to embarrass her more so, mystified and hurt, I too looked away. Then we pulled into the compound airlock and out again and she was lost to view.

The wheels made a purring sound upon the plastic roadway. Sleepee dream galleries blipped past as we made our way to the travel tube.

The walkways had their usual quota of Sleepees upon

them. Some of them gaped at our passage, others appeared not to see us. Why should they? They were probably trying to relive their sleepstate, having nothing to do but eat, breathe, defecate and wait for their stumber handout during the wakestate, after their task – whatever it was – had been carried out.

I was taken aback by their appearance, with their diminutive stature, grey skins, hollow eyes, sparse hair, grimly dull clothing.

Could I have looked like that only a few weeks ago? Would they all change as I had with a richer atmosphere, better nutrition and longer hours of consciousness? I could think of no reason why they should not, and I felt the anger growing inside me again.

Then I felt a dullness and I realized that the thin atmosphere outside the Texec compound was having its effect. I put the inhaler to my nostrils and wondered about the journey ahead.

I did not have long to wonder.

Helgon drove us into the tubeport and got off the trolley, beckoning me to follow him.

The tubeport was like any other airlock, only bigger and smellier. It was empty save for a travelcard scanner and a few chairs. It did not look to me like a place which Texecs enjoyed coming to. There was none of that grace and opulence which they bestowed upon communal places that they cherished.

Nothing I had seen so far would convince me that the Texecs relished the thought of travelling. Why had they told me that they did? Surely they knew that all they had to do was to tell me to travel and I'd travel, provided they gave me a good reason.

Perhaps that was the trouble. They didn't have a good reason.

Helgon operated the travelcard scanner and sauntered over towards a low part of the port where the wall bulged convexly as though it formed part of a cylinder which continued beyond the port's boundaries.

'This is where we get on,' said Helgon, tapping the door in this strange wall.

I went to it and tried the opening lever. Helgon laughed. 'You'd never shift that,' he said. 'It's inoperable until there's a capsule the other side. Just as well, too. If you opened that door now you would be sucked into the transportation cylinder and that would be very uncomfortable. There's a vacuum the other side of that door.'

'What for?' I said.

Helgon shook his head. 'You've a lot to learn,' he said. I had heard that before. He went on: 'The regions are connected by vacuum-filled transportation tubes for two reasons: it saves oxygen, and the travel capsules move quicker – much quicker – in a vacuum.'

'How quickly do they move?'

He thought for a minute. 'Well, putting it in terms you could understand, I would say . . . about two thousand times quicker than the trolley that got us here.'

I did some mental arithmetic. 'That's incredible. At that speed we would be across this region in . . . in . . .'

Helgon said it for me. 'Ninety seconds?'

'About that.'

'So how long is the journey?'

'Shouldn't take more than half an hour.'

My mental arithmetic that time told me more than figures. Great vistas of ignorance and inquiry opened up before me. Surely this travel time must mean that there must be many, many regions to bypass before our destination. More, indeed, than were known to exist.

And as always when I had an important question to put, I kept silent and resolved to find the answer for myself. Helgon appeared not to notice anything. There was a humming in the air and a faint tremor underfoot.

Then there was a deafening shriek, a vibration in the tubeport, a thundering and then a steady mechanical roar.

'Capsule's here,' said Helgon. 'The door will open in a minute. I should stand away, just in case. You never know.'

I noticed that he had gone towards the street entrance.

With a hiss and a thud, the door to the cylinder opened. I walked towards it and peered into the capsule. It was circular in section and about thirty feet long. The entrance was at one of the extremities of the device. I looked along its length. It contained a series of discs which as I watched them began to revolve on their axes from vertical to horizontal.

On the other side of their blank backs was a great cushion, about six feet long, set about with an arrangement of straps and harnesses to which a number of travellers were attached.

I looked round for Helgon. He waved me inside. 'Jump on a pad and strap yourself in,' he called. 'I'll be with you in a minute.'

An attendant appeared from the other end of the capsule and helped me choose a pad, showing me how to attach myself to it. He wore a guard's uniform and looked tired. If he noticed that I was a Sleepee he didn't show it. His fingers were deft as they handled the straps into position.

I was secure. I tried one of the metal-to-metal buckles. It would not budge. I was locked in.

Where was Helgon? I craned my neck to see if he had come aboard but could not see him. I shouted for him. The attendant came up, asked me what I wanted. I told him. He shook his head. 'You're the only one who has come on here,' he said, and walked away.

I gave up. I felt almost as though what happened to me were none of my business.

There was a whirring sound and the door at the end slid to.

Then the pad that I was on revolved until I was upright, facing the door end.

Behind me there was a roaring sound and suddenly I felt as though gravity were pulling me backwards instead of downwards. For several seconds this feeling persisted and grew stronger until my body had compressed the cushion on which I lay so that I was almost totally enveloped in it.

Then the pressure eased and gravity resumed its normal

direction. The noise was intense and the capsule lurched and shook as it went hurtling through the vacuum tube. I tried to think of all those regions we must be passing through, but the effort was too great.

Then the pad on which I was strapped again started to revolve. This time it went through 180 degrees, so that I was facing the rear, my head pointing downwards.

The resulting discomfort was of short duration, however, as it quickly gave way to another form.

Again the pull of gravity seemed to shift to my rear. Again I sank, many times my usual weight, into the cushion, and again this strange phenomenon ended, allowing gravity to resume its customary pull.

Once more the disc revolved until it was back in the horizontal. The door of the capsule was open.

'Here we are, then, Cubale,' said a voice. It was the attendant.

Fumbling with my straps I released myself, swung off the disc and stood. My head swam. I took a pace forward, staggered, put a hand on to the side of the capsule to help me stay upright, and made my way to the door.

I came out into a tubeport which was almost identical to the one I had left. A great disturbance in the tubeport told me the capsule was departing. Soon I was alone, just standing there, not knowing what to do.

'Phillips,' said a voice. I looked around but could see no one. 'Phillips,' said the voice again, tinny but commanding. 'Come over here, by the scanner.' I walked across. The voice was Dmitri's. It was one I was used to obeying. 'To your right, a little below eye-level. The optiaudio controls. See them? Focus me in.'

I adjusted the dials, and Dmitri's image grew in the wall. He was sitting in his dining room where I had left him. A guard was clearing the remains of the meal, I noticed. Gerda was nowhere in the picture.

'You enjoyed the trip?'

'No.' Texecs liked a show of defiance within limits. What

they couldn't bear were awkward questions. I didn't put any.

But I nearly did. 'Dmitri,' I began, making it sound as though I was going to ask him something. He licked his lips and his eyes flickered sideways. He was preparing himself to lie, although he didn't even know what it was going to be. He just thought a lie was going to be necessary.

I put him out of his misery. 'Dmitri,' I said. 'Where do I go from here?'

'After Cubale?'

'No, no,' I said laughing. 'I'll come back to you after Cubale. What I meant was, where do I go from the tube-port?'

Dmitri let out a hiss of air, though you couldn't see him doing it.

'Don't worry about a thing,' he said. 'There's someone coming to meet you. He'll be with you any second.'

He paused and stared past me out of the screen. 'In fact he's with you right now,' he said, and began to fade.

I turned round.

'Welcome to Cubale,' said the Texec. He did not smile.

'Thanks,' I said, smiling. I looked at him. The Texecs were right after all. Travel could be interesting.

The man was dark – not as dark as Marie, but with a skin that was nearer brown than grey. He wore a close-fitting garment that appeared to be without fastenings. It covered him from throat to ankle and wrist. His skull cap was as black as his body garment, and was scalloped so that his temples were exposed and his forehead partially covered with a point that anticipated the direction of his nose. His feet were clad in shoes of a shiny black substance, and upon the third finger of his ungloved left hand there was a golden ring which bore a red circular stone. Apart from this and a red circle of thread on his skullcap there was no adornment. He seemed young, and yet had an air of considerable authority.

'You're observant,' he said.

'It's something you Texecs have taught me,' I said.

55

'Maybe,' he said. 'I wouldn't know. I've never taught a Sleepee. You're the first one here – outside the herd, you know. So I don't know anything about Sleepees, part from their calorie intake, their breathing requirements, their stumber consumption, that sort of thing. Come on.' He spoke in the same way as Helgon.

He walked to the exit and shoved the door. It swung open. He walked through it, letting it swing back on me. I pushed it, and it swung on its hinges again and I passed through.

'What's your name?' I asked the man as I caught up with him.

'Magnon.'

'Mine's Phillips. It used to be . . . it used to be . . .' I felt stupid. I could not remember the name I had had as a Sleepee. Magnon did not seem to notice.

'Where are you taking me?'

'To your quarters, of course. I don't know what you are supposed to do down here, but you'll have to have some-where to live. And I don't suppose we could put you back in a dormy. Not now.'

'No, I don't suppose you could,' I said, terrified. I fought for the words. 'I mean, that's the whole point, isn't it? The Texecs got me out of the dormys because they thought I could be useful. They've taught me a lot. That's why they sent me here, to learn more.'

'Is it?'

'Yes.' I was beginning to feel trapped. Life was not easy in my home region, but at least I knew where I was. Here, I felt adrift. What was Cubale? Who was this Magnon? Why did he appear to be ignorant about me? Had no one told him?

'Can I get in touch with Dmitri?' I said.

'Who's Dmitri?' asked Magnon, without curiosity, pausing in his stride.

I felt hot and breathless, although the air was good. Magnon unlocked a street door and pushed it open. Within was a small, simply furnished room with a door at the other end.

56

No windows, none of the ornaments with which the Texecs at home used to decorate their homes.

'This is it, then,' said Magnon.

I walked in. 'Very nice,' I lied (although it was very nice compared to a dormy). 'What do I do now?'

'Suit yourself,' said Magnon, who stood in the doorway for an instant, regarding me with an expression almost approaching interest. Then he stepped back and slammed the door.

'But . . .' I ran to the door, turned the handle and pushed.

The door would not budge.

Finally I gave up hammering it, went to the bed and lay down, trying not to think.

I lay there for I do not know how long. Once I got up to urinate, and discovered that there was a lavatory and a washbasin, as well as a small food dispenser behind the door in the back of the room. And once I got up to peer through a small hole at eye height pierced through the main door.

Outside the corridor we had walked along was deserted. I wondered where all the Sleepees of Cubale went in wake-state. Then I went back to the bed and slept fitfully, finding myself disturbed from time to time by the sound of scratching and banging on the wall. Eventually it stopped, and I sank into a deep and refreshing slumber in the full glare of the room's light source.

6

WHEN I awoke I found that my mood of confusion and despair had given way to optimism, a sense which was not dispelled even by the forbidding presence of Magnon.

'Good day,' I said.

'Your people have been on to us again,' he replied.

'They've explained a bit more. Though I still can't understand why they wanted to get rid of you so quickly.' He looked at me oddly. 'Has there been some trouble with the women?'

My expression must have told him that I had no idea what he was talking about, and he went on: 'Ah, never mind. It's very inconvenient having you here, but we owe your people a favour or two, so I suppose we'd better do our best. It's all very strange. They seem to think very highly of you, although they wanted you out of the way in such a hurry. They asked me to teach you our system. So . . . you'd better come with me.'

I realized that I was extremely hungry. 'Do you mind if I eat first?'

Magnon shrugged. 'Don't take too long over it.'

The food dispenser did not work. I told Magnon. 'Haven't they given you a creditpass?' he asked. I shook my head. Sighing heavily, he handed me a small, cylindrical key. 'They ask a lot, your people,' he said. 'You'd better use this until we fix you up with one. But anything you use down here will be debited to their account, so you'd better not be too generous with yourself.'

'Thanks.'

I brandished Magnon's key at the apparatus and programmed for some synthabrek, a preparation light in fat and protein which I had come to favour for my first meal of the day.

The meal was finished in a few seconds, and I wiped the inside of the carton clean with my forefinger. 'What do I do with this?' I said.

"There's a district reprocesser down the corridor,' said Magnon. 'We'll pass it on our way.'

The scratching sound, as of metal against stone, had started again. I stopped to listen, hoping, for some reason, that Magnon had not heard it. 'Go on,' he said. I was relieved.

I was the first to leave the room and turned left, for some

reason assuming that we would retrace our steps towards the tubeport.

But Magnon, after closing the door with a bang, turned to the right, and began to stride away at a good pace. Startled, I wheeled round, and as I did so, dropped the empty synthabrek carton. Hurriedly stooping to pick it up, my gaze caught a glitter from the centre of the door next to mine.

It was there only momentarily, and then it vanished. But it took only a split second for me to realise that the glitter was from an eye.

I caught up with Magnon, and was happy that he did not speak for the next ten minutes, for I would have been unable to concentrate on his words.

In fact I was hardly aware of the direction in which he was taking me. The thoroughfares of Cubale were altogether less generous than what I had been used to, and for the most part were made up of corridors with low skies and seldom more than six feet across.

But there were few people about, and of those all were Texecs – invariably with skins of the same brown shade as Magnon's. They dressed similarly, too, although not always in the same colour. He was greeted by them with respect.

Eventually, he stopped.

We were in a corridor which was even dimmer than those we had passed through. There was no obvious source of illumination, and any that filtered through from the more brightly-lit thoroughfares at either end was quickly absorbed by the walls.

'I think you'll find us more efficient than your friends at home,' said Magnon. He turned to the wall, put his hand in a recess, and pulled a small lever. He nodded over his shoulder. 'Look,' he said.

Opposite, a section of the wall some fifty feet long rolled upwards to reveal a huge window beneath which was a great cavern crammed full of Sleepees, their naked skins glowing dully in the dim light.

'Highly concentrated Sleepee accommodation,' observed Magnon, his strange voice more animated. 'Thirty-six cubic feet per individual, a wakestate period of only one hour in five, as against your one in four, an unvarying low oxygen demand, small nutritional requirements, and so on.'

'Do they never leave?' I asked. Magnon shook his head. 'Only if they die,' he said. 'After all, what's the point? There's no room for them out here, and they wouldn't know what to do. Anyway the air would probably knock them out.'

I looked at Magnon. What he said could well be true. In the public places of Cubale, the atmosphere was of a uniformly high quality, whereas at home, only the Texec compound had this service. This meant . . .

'Do all the Sleepees live like this in Cubale?' I asked.

'Sure do,' said Magnon. 'There wouldn't be room for them otherwise.'

The discrepancy between the living standards of the Texecs and the Sleepees at home had made me indignant but this was beyond forgiveness.

I said nothing.

Magnon was explaining to me that the Sleepee Caverndormys were all self-contained with their own internal reprocessing plants for nutrition, water and air.

He manipulated some controls that lay behind a panel in the wall. 'Look,' he said, pointing into the cavern.

Following the direction of his finger I saw a trough-like device, some twenty feet in length, supported at each end by a tall box.

As I looked, the trough began to move, running in a belt from one of the boxes to the other. And then, as it moved, a pipe leading out of one of the boxes gave out a black viscous substance which dropped into the moving trough.

Then one or two of the Sleepees began to shuffle slowly towards the device. For a minute or two they stood before it, and then put a hand into the trough, cupping it against the flow.

Within seconds, the hand that had been in the trough contained a pile of the substance, and its owner would withdraw from the device to eat what he held.

'That's the unit processor,'' said Magnon. "Neat, hey?'

I was silent, as in twos or threes, the Sleepees stumbled towards their feeding machine, took a handful of nutriment, and then retired to feed.

'Most efficient,' I said, feeling sick.

I lost all sense of time and place as I stood there gazing into Magnon's automated pit, watching the Sleepees go about the process of what they thought was life. My eyes filled with tears.

Magnon was talking to me. 'I said, do you want to go in there to see?'

'Oh, er, yes. Of course,' I said.

'Then grab this.' Magnon gave me an air enricher. I slipped the mask over my face and followed Magnon to the far end of the window and into the first hermetic door I had seen since coming to Cubale.

The Sleepees seemed unaware of our entry. Their eyes were vacant, their mouths slack. When Magnon was absorbed in the functioning of a piece of equipment I turned my back on him and removed the oxygen mask. The air was not too thin to carry the stench I had expected.

And the heat was hard to bear. I was tempted to remove my clothes and wander about naked, like my fellow Sleepees.

But Magnon, who was working on some machinery, was covered from throat to ankle. I felt that if he could stand it, so must I.

Observing the Sleepees move about sluggishly in the dim red light of the cell, I was at a loss to discover any purpose in what they did.

They seemed not to seek pleasure, nor even relief from discomfort; there was no apparent communication between themselves and they were totally uncommunicative. If one

61

happened to touch another in passing, neither would show any awareness of the encounter. Even those not asleep were mostly seated or lying down; those who did move about did so only for a short time.

I wondered if they were capable of speech, or even thought.

'Enjoying yourself?' It was the lugubrious Magnon, turned cheery in these surroundings.

I did not have to smile, for my mouth was covered with the oxygen mask. 'Yes thanks.' My reply sounded muffled to me, but he seemed satisfied.

'Well, I'm through. You can stay for a while if you like.' He looked at me hard. I felt he was offering a challenge I should not refuse.

'Thanks.' Even as I said it I regretted it. I wanted to get out of that evil hole as soon as I could, but something compelled me to stay.

Magnon seemed pleased. 'All right. I've got another cell up the road to look at. I'll come back in half an hour.'

His departure went unnoticed by the Sleepees, as our arrival had done. He went up the steps. There was a boom and hiss as the hermetic door opened and closed, and Magnon was gone, leaving me alone with the Sleepees.

I checked myself. I was almost beginning to think of the Sleepees as 'them' instead of as 'us'. It was a trap into which I could easily fall in Cubale.

Sauntering among the seated and supine forms in the cell, I tried vainly to seek out a face that looked intelligent. Finally I decided on a little man sitting by himself, on a patch of floor by the mechanical trough. Although he betrayed no positive signs of intelligence, his eyes looked less dead than those of the majority.

I sat down beside him.

'Can you talk?' I asked.

He looked at me, and looked away again.

'Can you understand me?' I persisted.

Once more he looked at me. 'Uh,' he said.

'Then you know I am talking to you,' I said.

He waved his hand from his wrist in a gesture of indifference, or contempt, or both.

'Look at me,' I said.

He did so.

'I am a Sleepee, too,' I said. 'And look at me. I am bigger than you, eat better, have a more interesting life, sleep in a cell of my own, have soft seats to sit on and beds to lie on. . .'

His eyes had flickered with interest when I said that I ate better than he.

'Here.' There was a bar of substichoc in one of my pockets. It was battered, and the wrapping was torn, but he took it with a grabbing movement that was the quickest example of co-ordination I had seen since I had come into the cell.

He munched in a slow and furtive manner, glancing occasionally from side to side. But most of the time his gaze was downcast.

I watched him eat, and looked for signs of higher intelligence. Dribble fell from his mouth to the floor. He did not wipe his mouth. Suddenly I took away the substichoc.

His hand followed mine as it quickly withdrew the delicacy from him, but once I had taken it beyond his reach, he let the hand fall into his lap, allowing himself a quick glance of reproach in my direction.

He showed something like eagerness when I gave it back to him, however, and I said: 'Would you like some more?'

'Yuh.'

So he had not entirely lost the powers of speech.

'I'll give you some more if you talk to me.'

He did not react.

'How long have you been here?'

He shrugged.

'Do you like it here?'

He shrugged.

'Would you like to leave?'

He shrugged, and then shook his head, shrugged again.

'Look, I was like you once.' This wasn't entirely true, but

it would do. 'If you left this place, you could be like me. You could have lots of nutriment like I just gave you. Just tell me what I want to know. Just tell me anything.'

He was beginning to be restless. Then he stood up. My heart beat faster. He took a slow pace forward, and then another one. He looked at me as though inviting me to follow him. I went after him as he made for the rows of bunks where his co-inhabitants were. He peered at several rows before apparently finding what he sought. The Sleepee leaned over one of the bunks and shoved. Inch by inch, he pushed the sleeping figure over. At last he seemed satisfied, and crawled into the bit of room he had made for himself.

Before closing his eyes, he said quite clearly: 'Dream now'. Within seconds he was asleep.

In despair I turned away and walked along the rows of bunks, piled on top of one another in threes, each giving room for three or four supine figures.

I paused to allow a Sleepee to roll half-off one of the bunks and sit, feet on floor, elbows on knees, head in hands. It was a female and her breasts hung from her, swaying slightly.

As Sleepees went she had generous protuberances, and I put out a hand to touch one. It yielded, and swung back as I withdrew my hand. She did not look up.

For a moment I lost count of time as I stood there, watching her return slowly to consciousness.

Then I felt a quick surge of panic and tried to look at my watch. I pressed its sides and the dial lit up. Magnon should have picked me up fifteen minutes ago!

Fighting the urge to break into a run, I went to the door and banged it. But the sound was immediately lost in its mass. I went to the window and looked out into the black corridor outside. It was so dimly lit that I could see little.

But I was sure that no Texec was out there. I banged on the glass, but the sound was immediately lost in the vacuum that lay between the two skins of the window.

'Magnon!' I shouted. One or two Sleepees stirred on their bunks. Others, awake, looked at me briefly.

64

I fought to remain calm. Deliberately I walked away from the door and sat on a step. After a few minutes I rose, and walked around the cavern. Where could he have gone? What had delayed him?

In vain I sought some way of communicating with the outside. There was nothing. I did find a large stone, which had come away from one of the steps. I picked it up and took it over to the door, where I left it. The time had not come for trying to smash through the window but it might yet.

After a while I began to feel hungry and thirsty, but I was determined to refrain for as long as I could from drinking or eating at the sources used by the Sleepees. From either their food or their drink, or both, they received their supply of stumber. I had no desire to reduce my wakestate to a mere six hours a day. Besides, once I started taking stumber again, there was no telling how rapidly I would backslide into the Sleepee condition.

Where could Magnon be?

Cursing myself for giving away the substichoc, I kept as still as I could, and forced myself to relax.

My oxygen bottle was beginning to run low, so I turned it off and braved the thin and rancid air of the cavern. Soon I felt an overwhelming desire to sleep. My head rolled, my eyes closed and I lost consciousness.

How long I slept I do not know, but I awoke in acute discomfort. My bones creaked as I tried to stand, and I rubbed my buttocks to restore the flow of blood.

I yearned for things of the body – for comfort, for food, for good air, above all for drink. All round in the red-lit cavern I could see drinking fountains inviting me to quench my thirst.

At least comfort of a sort was within my reach. Like the little Sleepee before me, I made my way along the rows of bunks, looking for one with some room.

One, in the corner, held only three bodies, while most of the others contained at least six. It was on the top row, some five feet above floor level, and I hauled myself upon it and lay down.

I was hungry, thirsty and, despite having slept, exhausted in the third-grade atmosphere.

As soon as my head touched the surface of the bunk my mind's eye perceived water in great quantities: covering an entire habitat in a still, flat stretch; water falling enormously from a great wall into a boiling pit, rushing over stones, spurting up from the floor in a great jet to cover me with its life-giving spray.

My tongue clove to the roof of my mouth and in agony I lifted my head. Immediately the images disappeared. They returned the instant my head touched the bunk again.

I realized what was happening, but did not care. So long as I did not take their stumber I would survive my sojourn on the dream-activated bunks.

The flight of time became indistinct. The figures on my watch lost their meaning; after a while I no longer looked at them. I remained aware of my existence but was unable to tell whether I was conscious or not.

The drinking fountains beckoned me. Whichever way I turned there would be the sight of one, dripping with water, or of the bent back of a Sleepee sucking at their offerings.

Forcing myself not to drink became, somehow, no longer an exercise of the will. It was a condition of existence, a price to be paid for the privilege of life's continuance.

As I lay on the bunk, the images of water that it sent into my brain became ever more luxuriant, while my body's demands for drink grew shriller.

Then, somehow, I found myself at one of the fountains, gulping down the liquid that came so generously from it. My wits revived as the water coursed on its life-giving way through my parched system.

I sprang back from the fountain, appalled at my self-betrayal. And, as I did so, I heard my name.

'Phillips.'

It was Magnon. He called again.

'Are you there, Phillips? Or perhaps I should call you Jim again?'

He chuckled.

'Where are you Jim, my little Sleepee? Are you all tired now you're taking your stumber again? Are you sleeping sweetly, Sleepee?'

He was moving along the bunks, shining a flashlight into the faces of the occupants. So my confinement here had been deliberate!'

I went back, as quietly as I could, to the bunk where I had been lying, grabbed the enricher outfit, put the mask to my face, turned the tap, took a good lungful. For an instant I thought I would faint. Then my head stopped spinning and I found that I could think again.

I dodged across to another row of bunks, dived into one of them and crawled over the unprotesting bodies to the other side, away from Magnon, who was now examining some of the Sleepees who were in wakestate.

He was clearly perturbed. He would have thought me easy to find, as the only Sleepee present with clothes on.

As he examined one side of the cavern, I ran up the other towards the door. My piece of rock was still there.

Glancing over my shoulder to ensure that Magnon was not looking in my direction, I darted forward to retrieve the stone and then went back to the row of bunks.

He was beginning to make his way down another row. Selecting the end furthest from him, I tried to find a space on the top row. Failing to do this, I grabbed a Sleepee by the arm and pulled her off, catching her as she fell, and stuffing her into a lower row.

Then I ripped off my clothes, left them in a pile on the floor with the breathing equipment, and climbed up into the bunk taking the rock with me. I rolled the unconscious Sleepees across and crawled over to the edge.

There I lay, facing outwards, knees bent up, head bowed forward, arms between legs, knees concealing hands – and the rock held between them.

67

He had not noticed any of this, amid all the comings and goings of the Sleepees.

Magnon approached. He inspected the next row but one. Then the next one.

I allowed him to recognize my pale skin first. Then I rammed the stone into his oxygen mask.

He fell backwards on to the floor. I leaped off the bunk and on top of him. The breath came out of his body in an expressionless groaning shout which made even some of the Sleepees look round.

I knelt on his chest with the stone raised above my head, ready to smash into his face once more, but he was unconscious.

His clothes fell away after I activated the garment fastener demagnetising button at his collar, and I pulled them completely from him. I tried to rip his one-piece, but failed. So I turned him over and, after going through the pockets, with one leg of the pants tied his arms together and with the other, his legs.

I dragged him over to a bunk and put him on to one of the low-levels, attaching him, with the spare arms of his garment, firmly to it.

As Magnon lay there, semi-prone, I regarded his large body. A thin trickle of blood, black in the cavern's redness, came from one corner of his mouth and dripped on to his chest, but I did not think that he was badly hurt.

He was almost twice the size of the biggest Sleepee male in the cavern; his limbs were abundantly covered with muscle and sinew and his large chest had a generous amount of flesh to adorn it.

You could not see his ribs, except the lower ones.

I knew I would never have a physique like his: to attain that sort of thing you have to breathe and eat like a Texec from infancy.

I breathed into his air-enricher, smelt the blood, and then went to his clothes and emptied out the pockets and the satchel he always carried.

Among his belongings was a flask, as I knew there would

be. Hands trembling, I unscrewed the stopper and drank. When it was empty I took the flask over to the drinking fountain and filled it. Then I returned to Magnon, opened his mouth, and poured some liquid in. He swallowed, choked, spluttered and came to. He tried to rise, failed, grew furious, struggled against his bonds, gave up, leant back and groaned.

'My head,' he said.

'Drink this,' I said. 'It will help.'

He looked at me half in bewildered suspicion but drank nevertheless.

'Get it all down you,' I said. 'It's the only way.' Obediently he gulped.

'No more,' he mumbled.

'Drink,' I said. And once more the flask was empty. He belched, shook his head, blinked his eyes and looked puzzled.

'What . . . what happened?' he asked. And then, immediately, 'You!' he said.

'Yes, Magnon,' I said. 'Surprised?'

He said nothing. Instead he grunted as he pulled against his bonds once more.

'You wanted me to revert to this,' I said, waving an arm to indicate the cavern. 'You despise all Sleepees, and to have to accept one on terms almost of equality infuriated you. Am I right?'

'Yes, you *thing*.' He snarled the words. I smiled at him.

'You thought if you left me here long enough I would drink the stumber-treated water and eat the drugged nutrition, and I would sleep, and go into dreamstate and go back to my original condition. No.'

'Yes, damn you,' he said. 'You will do this anyway. It's just a matter of time. I was simply trying to accelerate an inevitable process. It's a waste of resources letting you live like a Texec. You're no good to anyone, little Sleepee. Now untie me.'

I laughed. 'Untie you?' I asked. 'When I went to all that

trouble trying you up? Oh, no, Magnon. You're going to stay where you are for a while.'

His expression was changing. It occured to him for the first time, I think, that he was no longer in charge of events. As he shook off the muzziness caused by the blow, he was becoming better able to work things out for himself. He couldn't have liked it much.

He made an attempt at conciliation. 'I'm . . . sorry, Phillips,' he said. He tried to make it sound easy, but the effort nearly killed him. He went on: 'Look, I didn't know what I was saying just now. I was still dizzy from that blow. I didn't mean it. And I don't blame you for hitting me, either. I didn't realise you'd take it so hard. I thought you'd be happier back with the Sleepees. . .' I just looked at him. The words dried up.

He tried again. 'Aw, come on . . . please?' he said.

I didn't move. 'I see,' I said. 'You thought I'd be happier?'

He nodded, eagerly. 'Yes, yes I really did. I can see that I was wrong, but . . .'

'You'll soon find out the joys of being a Sleepee,' I said. 'And then you'll know whether you were right or wrong.'

His eyes widened. 'You see – you've been drinking stumber water. You have . . .' I tapped his empty flask, '. . . about a litre inside you.'

'Ah, never, never . . .' I could see the veins standing out on his throat and temples as he pulled at the bonds again.

'Tell me,' I said. 'As soon as your head touches a bunk you're in dreamstate – right?'

He ignored me. 'How come?' He stayed silent. I kicked him, not too hard, in the crutch. He moaned and tried to pull his knees up. 'How come?'

'Static circuit. It's all activated. It saves you having to plug 'em in.' He spoke in little grunts. His face was shiny with sweat.

'One more thing before you nod off.' He looked at me. 'You'd better tell me how to run this place. It's in both our interests. If anything goes wrong, then your colleagues will

70

have to investigate, and I'll be in trouble. But you could be dead.' He looked at me again, even more astonished.

I laughed. 'Not me. I wouldn't kill you. I'm thinking of them. The Sleepees. Deprive them of their full stumber ration and they could wreck the place – and you with it. You know I'm right.'

'I was so wrong about you,' said Magnon. 'I almost like you now. But that won't stop me from killing you once I get a chance.'

'You won't ever get out unless you tell me,' I said.

I had fun watching him try to stay awake, as he watched me eat his packaged meal. Then he fell asleep. I adjusted his tethers so that his head made a good contact with the activated surface of the bunk.

From time to time he twitched.

They always do.

7

I PULLED my clothes on quickly and then attended to the nutrition reprocessing machines and the atmosphere regulating plant. The water supply stumber reserves needed topping up so I took his key, waved it at the storeroom door and took out the required amount. The smell of the drug drifted into my nostrils and I was vividly reminded of luxury – of a green island in a warm lake, of a limitless sky. And of a crack in the sky. I shook away the memories and got through the work as quickly as I could.

Calculating that Magnon would remain asleep for at least another twelve hours, I decided to return to my cell for some Texec nutrition, some unassisted breathing, some natural sleep, and some thought.

I was very tired, very hungry, very unsure.

Before I left, I put Magnon's belongings into his satchel, and put the satchel into the storeroom. I took only his key. If any Texec were to find me in possession of Magnon's goods, then I would be in trouble. But I had to have the key.

The walk back to the cell was longer than I thought it would be, but I had little difficulty in remembering it. I remembered Magnon telling me that Cubale was built on a system of right-angled intersections, so it was hard to get lost for long.

My cell door was still open and I walked in to find it looking just the same as when I had left it hours, or days, or whatever it was ago. I was surprised. For some strange, subconscious reason, I had expected it to be different.

I closed the door behind me and went straight to the nutriment dispenser.

Grabbing the meal – I didn't even notice what sort it was – I staggered to the little bed, sat down, gobbled the nutriment, lay down and almost immediately lost consciousness.

I woke, just once, to set the caller on my watch, and then I became oblivious again.

I woke with a start to see a plastic panel peeling back from the wall. I leapt from the bed, grabbed a stool and sprinted across to the opposite wall, prepared to beat off my attackers.

'Come on, help me through,' they said, and I blinked the sleep from my eyes to see a girl's head, arms and shoulders sticking through the hole.

'Just take my hands and heave,' she said. 'Come on, I'm squeezing the life out of my tits. Ouch.'

Bewildered, I helped the girl. Getting her hips through the hole was most difficult, and she obviously found it very uncomfortable, but she insisted on coming through. I didn't ask her why; I just helped.

Gently, I eased her to the floor. She stood there for a while, laughing and rubbing her flanks and buttocks.

'Well,' she said finally. 'Thanks.'

72

I looked at her. She was no taller than I was. She had straight thick hair and a broad face, with high cheekbones. She was plump and had a nice smile. I liked her. I smiled back. Then I looked at my watch, then I smiled again.

'Why didn't you come through the door?' I asked. She laughed some more. 'You really are a funny man.'

'No. I'm not.' I said.

She looked at me. 'Yes, I think you are. You really *are* a funny man,' she said. 'Didn't you know you were locked in?'

'Well, I was,' I said. 'But I'm not now.' And I went to the door and opened it. 'Are you?'

'Hold it,' she said, and ran out of the door into the corridor. Then she stopped and thought, and ran back in, slamming the door behind her.

'Crazy,' she said. 'These are retribution cells. They're always locked. I've been hacking away at a fault in my wall for days to find a way out. Why isn't yours locked? And if it's open, why don't you go home?'

I sat on the bed, my thoughts reeling.

'I didn't know,' I said. 'I haven't been here long. This is where they put me when I arrived. I didn't know it was a retribution cell. I thought it was just somewhere they put their guests. I live here. This is home.'

'You've done nothing wrong?' I shook my head. 'Well, you poor little fellow.'

Then I told her my story – about how I had been a Sleepee, and how the Texecs in my native region had singled me out for education and development because they thought I would be a help and how, suddenly, they had sent me to Cubale, ostensibly to learn something more about the world, but in fact it now seemed into captivity.

She listened to my story in silence. When I had finished her eyes were filled with tears. 'The Texecs . . . I'm one of them, but they are horrible, horrible,' she said. 'You poor creature.' She put her arms around me and made me lie down. I could taste tears as she put her face to mine.

I felt strange. Confused, yet comfortable. The odd and

73

enigmatic feelings which had been coming to me from time to time recently came again, stronger than ever before.

After a while, she spoke. 'Now I must tell you why I am here, dear Phillips,' she said. 'It's because I'm a whore. Well, they don't mind that . . . but, well, we were a bit mad I suppose . . . we tried to go with a Sleepee, just to see.' She looked at me. 'You don't understand?'

'No.'

'I thought maybe you didn't. Well.' She undid my suit and put her hand down to my groin. 'You're a male, you see.' I felt it growing and swelling down there, and felt terrified and excited at the same time. And proud of something, but I didn't know what.

'And then,' she said. 'I'm a female.'

'I know,' I croaked.

'You don't,' she said, and put my hand between her legs, where it lay still. 'Go on, feel,' she said.

I had always known there was a difference. That about half the world were male and half female. And that they were different shapes. It was something everybody took for granted, and nobody discussed.

But nobody ever asked questions about anything. Not Sleepees, anyway.

And my hand and fingers, now moving eagerly across this strange, small area of damp and inviting flesh, discovered for me a new universe.

'I never knew . . . I never knew. Why is it like this?' I whispered. She kicked off her suit and helped me out of mine, saying nothing. We lay on the bed for a moment.

'Come,' she said. 'Feel the rest of me.'

She had a body not unlike mine in some ways but different in others. It was smoother and rounder. The texture of the skin was finer and most of her was softer. But the differences weren't that great apart from . . . down there.

The tactile qualities of another's body had never interested me before. With so many other things to learn from life, why was this lesson the most interesting of all?

74

I asked her.

'Don't ask, don't ask,' she said. She, too, was excited. I could tell. Her eyes were half-closed but glittering. Her face was shiny. Her breath came quickly. Her voice was hoarse.

'Come,' she said again. Somehow I found myself on top of her, with her legs to either side of mine.

'Come, come, come,' she said, and guided me into her.

It was then that I knew, as I moved about, hesitantly at first and then too eagerly and then with care. My ecstacy mingled with a growing bubble of disquiet which enlarged and threatened and burst as I did.

I slid off her and on to my back and beat my temples with the heels of my hands. She rolled round so that she was looking down on to me. I pushed with my forearm against her breasts and she fell back.

Groaning, I crawled from the bed to the floor and lay there for a moment, savouring its chill. There was a blackness encircling my vision and a roaring pulse inside my skull.

I realized she was talking to me. She gave me a link back to reality. Her voice came to me across the void and gave strength to my enfeebled reason.

'What's wrong?' I echoed her question, looked into her sadness. 'It's just that . . . now I know what my people, the Sleepees, are forbidden. It's what we did, isn't it?'

She nodded. 'Yes. I just didn't think – I didn't realize that you wouldn't know . . . *anything*. I just thought you hadn't done it before. I thought that's what made you so, so . . .'

'Inexpert?'

'Yes. Inexpert. That's it partly. I just didn't know you didn't know.' She was weeping now. I wept too. Then I put her back on to the bed and drove into her with a lust sharpened by discovery and an ancient anger newly found.

Afterwards we lay quietly, a little apart, hands touching. I felt unreal.

'When I first started cutting the wall I was hoping to get

75

to an empty cell and an unlocked door,' she said. 'I was disappointed when you came. But I thought if I couldn't have freedom then at least I could have you. But now I'm positively glad about you – you're pretty good considering you haven't had much practice.'

'Have you?'

'Have I what?'

'Had much practice?'

'Lots. I told you I was a whore, didn't I?'

'Is that what whore means – a girl who's had lots of practice?'

She laughed. 'In a way,' she said. 'It really means I like it more than most, and I take it when I can. They wouldn't mind if I was a man.' She pouted.

'Depends what sort of man.'

'Yes. I know.'

We lay in silence for a while.

'Why did you want to do it with a Sleepee?'

'Because . . . it was something people didn't do. We wanted to find out if it was possible. They say the Sleepees can't, but when I asked the other girls why not, they said they didn't know. So we thought we'd just find out.'

'We?'

'Me and Helgon. But you wouldn't know him, would you?'

Confinement for the female, I thought, and exile for the male. Useful for Lemington, too.

'So you went into a cavern?'

'Yes. I sneaked in behind a Texec on maintenance, hid behind a bunk, took my clothes off and just waited until he'd gone. Poo.' She wrinkled her nose.

'Poo?'

'*Awful.* I took a little air enricher with me, but I was hardly adequate. Anyway, I hung around, hoping one of the males would make a move because – well you know, I think I've got more than most of the Sleepee girls . . .'

'Have you?'

'Well, take a look round next time you go to a cavern . . .

76

Anyway, nobody even looked at me. So I picked out the best specimen I could find and tried to make out with him. It was impossible. I thought maybe it was me – you know, the smell, working under difficult conditions – I wasn't at my best. And then I noticed.'

'What?'

'Well, there I was in a huge room with about a thousand people in it, all naked and none of them doing it. I mean, get a roomful of Texecs like that and they would all be at it.'

'Would they?'

'Yes. They're always doing it. Some, like me, more than others, it's true. And then, most of them have one partner whom they keep for years. Sometimes for ever. But that doesn't stop them doing it with others as well.'

I thought of Dmitri and old Gerda.

She went on : 'So then I knew it really was true.'

'What?'

'Well, that Sleepees don't do it. That's why they are Sleepees. Helgon told me he had a female, but she didn't actually do anything, so that didn't count.'

'And now,' I said, 'you know once again that what you learned is wrong.'

She looked at me. 'M'm. You're still a Sleepee, aren't you? And there's nothing wrong with you.'

'Not now.'

'No, not now. What's the difference?'

I shrugged. 'I'm still the same person. Before, I ate as poorly as all the other Sleepees, breathed the same air, slept as long ... perhaps it's just a lack of stimulus.'

'Maybe so. But why did you sleep so long?'

'Well, because when a Sleepee is asleep, he dreams. His dreams are his life. He wakes only to prepare his body for sleep, really.'

'I see. But that doesn't really answer my question. Why do they sleep? And why do they dream so?'

'Oh, that. Well, that's this drug, stumber. All Sleepees

77

take it. It makes them sleep – and it makes them receptive to the dream stimuli.'

'Stumber, stumber.' She thought. 'Stumber,' she said. 'I remember. My sister couldn't sleep once, and they gave her stumber. She was older than me, but I remember – it helped her sleep, but she said it put her off sex as well. Stumber. I know – sterile slumber. See? Wait.' She closed her eyes. 'I'm trying to remember.' I waited. 'Now I have it: they distributed the stumber to the Sleepees because – what was it now – they were hoping to bring the consumption cycle down to safety level . . .' This last phrase was delivered as though by rote.

She opened her eyes. They were very dark brown. She laughed. 'I don't know what it means really. I just remember them talking about it when I was very young. That's what someone said.'

I felt confused. I knew even less than she the meaning of her words. But they sounded bad. I did know now, though, the essential difference between a Sleepee and a Texec. The Sleepee had his dreams. The Texec had his sex.

But if the Texecs gave the Sleepees their sleep and their dreams to keep them quiet, why did they not permit them their sex as well – or even instead?

'What's a sister?' I asked her.

'Well, she's a girl with the same parents as yourself,' she said.

'What are parents?' I asked.

8

I RAN to the cavern, fearing that Magnon would be totally recovered from his dose of stumber. I had left him longer than I had meant to, but I found him sullen-eyed and stupid when I got there.

78

It was easy to feed him the impregnated nutriment which I scooped out of the automatic trough, and he seemed glad of the drink I offered him from the fountain.

I looked for the stone I had hit him with before and kept it close by me while I untied his bonds. There was no need for me to worry. Being restrained for so long – about fourteen hours – had temporarily paralyzed his muscles.

'Sleep well?' I asked.

He spoke dully, but his voice had a faraway song in it, which I recognized. Sleepees recollecting a dreamstate which had given them more pleasure than usual always spoke like this.

'I flew,' he said. 'I was a great white bird skimming through limitless atmosphere, cold and rich. And it was bright, brighter than any daytime luxury level of illumination. A great blinding source of light hung in the sky, which was a deep and perfect and intangible blue. Beneath me was a stretch of water, blue and green and flecked with white, stretching away to infinity, and I felt free and exalted and I passed through this environment, regulating at will my level above this water, proceeding through the pure chill about me . . .'

I left him talking. His command of language was better than that of any Sleepee I knew, but his commitment to the dreamstate was no less complete for all that.

And so the pattern for the next few weeks of my life was set. I left my retribution cell once a day to run furtively through the corridors of Cubale to attend to Magnon's caverns. Terrified of the consequences of refusing to co-operate with me he always told me what had to be done.

Back in my cell, Gnofina – for that was the name of the whore – was always waiting, always pleased to see me. I could never discover why.

I learned from Magnon all he knew about Cubale, which was a lot, and the rest of the world which was a little, and Gnofina, because she liked it, taught me all she knew about sex.

All of Magnon's privileges were mine: his creditpass key

79

was in my possession. I could have taken all that Cubale had to offer a master Texec, but I did not. All I took was Magnon's one-piece, which Gnofina altered so that it fitted me.

Caution prevailed, and I chose to remain where I was in the retribution cells with Gnofina.

So I felt safe. Only when a wrongdoer was delivered to his cell, or another was released, was there any activity in the retribution corridor. And I was able to keep myself out of the way when Texecs did come.

Just once, overcome by curiosity, I made my way to Magnon's apartment. From the outside it appeared larger than the caverns which housed a thousand Sleepees – and from what I could see of the inside as I walked hurriedly by, that was pretty luxurious.

The apartment appeared empty, and I wondered if Magnon had anyone living with him. If he had, doubtless she – or he – would be missing him – but could she initiate a search? The authorities would note that Magnon's caverns were being run normally, and would assume that Magnon was doing the running.

But if there were a search, they would look in the caverns only if they suspected that Magnon was ill, or had been injured. And they would be looking for a fully-dressed Texec, not a naked Sleepee.

So I felt safe.

Or rather I felt that I would be safe for the time being. But I knew that this could not go on for ever. I did not want it to go on for ever, either. I wanted action. I wanted to wreck the whole obscene system of habitat living. And I wanted to do it in a hurry.

One line of my attack would have its effect eventually, but how extensive that effect would be I did not know: it might be catastrophic for the Texecs; it might merely present them with a minor irritation.

But it was a start. Bahni was a start.

Bahni was the little Sleepee I had approached when I first went into Magnon's cavern. After some days of calling there, I realized that my first instincts had been correct; Bahni was a cut above the other Sleepees. The effect of stumber coupled with the foul air and the low-grade reprocessed sewage he was given for nutriment was for some reason less stupefying on him than on his fellows.

So I put him on his own. I put him in a middle-tier bunk with sheets of plastic attached to the upper and lower supports so that he could not escape. I made a small door so that I could get to him and give him his food and drink which I brought to him every day from my cell.

After a few days of this, he showed some distress, but was able to express himself far better than when I had first seen him. 'I want dream. Go back to . . . pink caves . . .' he said.

I knew how he felt. I tried to be kind. 'Well, perhaps you'll go back there one day,' I said. 'Meanwhile, try this.' And I gave him an air enricher. 'Go on,' I said, 'breathe through it, like me.' And I got alongside him on the bunk to show him how to operate the instrument.

His hand, shaking, reached out for it. He put it to his face, looking at me over the top of the mask. 'Go on,' I said. 'Breathe in.' The sounds of inhalation and exhalation reassured me. They grew stronger and more regular by the second.

'Good, good,' I said. He grunted. 'Go on,' I said. 'It'll make a man of you.' Then he was on top of me, his fingers round my throat.

His attack had caught me by surprise, although it shouldn't have. I wriggled, and tried to throw him off. The space was confined and I found it difficult to manoeuvre. My arms were in an awkward position, and they lacked leverage as I tried to prise his hands away. My breath was rattling in my throat, and the cavern started spinning. I was rapidly getting weaker, partly as a result of the little air Bahni permitted through my windpipe being the foul air of the cavern: he had knocked off my breathing mask.

I was aware of sinking into a great tube. The blackness was relieved by bright lights which illuminated nothing.

81

Then, somehow, I sensed that his grip was loosening. I made another attempt to shake him off. I got out from under him and rolled on top. His body was slippery with sweat. One of his arms was stretched out of the little door.

He was struggling with something that was not me. I placed a forearm across his throat and eased my feet towards the opening.

Slowly, avoiding his awkwardly-held arm, for I did not want to injure him, I backed out from his improvised cage.

'All right, you can let go now,' I said.

Once released, Bahni's arm hung limply from the aperture. The fight had gone out of him for the time being. I shoved the arm back into the aperture and slammed and carefully bolted the door.

Turning to my rescuer, I said: 'What made you do it?'

But Magnon was unable or unwilling to articulate. Head and shoulders above the Sleepees around him, he made a strange figure as he slouched away to the trough, scooped out a handful of nutriment and went to a bunk where he lay down and quietly ate. I might not have been there.

What instinct forced him to my rescue? Was there in his stumber-befuddled being the feeling that his survival depended still on me? Was he as a Texec driven by loyalty to the person in charge? Or like the Texecs in my home region, did he intuitively feel that I was something worth rescuing?

Even now, I feel that I only half-know the answer to these questions, and Magnon will never tell me.

'What do you want?' It was Bahni. 'What do you *want*?'

I turned to his prison, and spoke through the aperture. 'I want to help you,' I said.

'What do you want?' he said.

'I – want – to – help – you,' I said.

'Help?' he said.

'Soon,' I said. 'Soon.'

'Soon?' he said.

I sighed, and turned away. The job would need much patience.

After what seemed ages, but was in fact little more than a fortnight, I felt that Bahni was ready.

Gnofina and I waited for the middle hour, when most of the Texecs were resting and made our way to Bahni's cavern.

The door swung open with a hiss and we stepped inside. We paused to allow our eyes to become used to the gloom.

'How can they live in this?' wheezed Gnofina. 'They don't. It's not living,' I said. Then I called.

'Bahni. Bahni!'

'Here. No. Over here.'

'Well, come here then.'

'No.'

'Why not?'

'Her.'

From behind the bunk a bare arm flashed, pointing towards Gnofina, and then disappeared again.

I started: 'What do you mean?' when Gnofina interrupted.

'He's shy.' I looked at her. She gave a little shrug. She said: 'Well, I'm a stranger. A woman. He doesn't want to meet me in the nude. Give him his clothes.'

'Ah, don't be ridiculous,' I said. 'After all, he's only . . .'

'Now then,' she said. 'So are you. And would you. . . .?'

'No. I wouldn't,' I said, and went towards Bahni with the parcel of clothes I had been carrying.

After his attack on me, Bahni had made rapid progress. I had been able fairly quickly to have rudimentary conversation with him, and soon after was able to prove to him that there *was* a world outside the cavern, that the wake-state need not necessarily be intolerable.

He developed a sense of curiosity. With what seemed to me an astonishing ease he regained the facility for intelligible communication.

He found, as I had, that the desire for stumber intensified after it had been withheld for a period, but as his intellectual and spiritual powers reasserted themselves he regarded the overcoming of his desire as a worthwile challenge.

As I spoke to him about the Texecs and the Sleepees, and the system imposed by the Texecs upon the majority his indignation sprouted. I hoped that it would flower into the burning hatred that mine had – but I could not expect that to happen straight away.

But at least, when I first put my plans to him, he took them up with enthusiasm. I was delighted.

'Right,' I had said. 'We'll get you out of here as soon as we can.'

I gave him the clothes. He grabbed them and with hands that trembled, clumsily started to pull them on.

'Here, let me help you.'

'Thanks. I used to be able to dress myself. But it was a long time ago. I don't know how long ago, but a long time ago.'

'I know, I know. Then they took it all away.'

'Yes. How do I look?'

'Beautiful.'

We grinned at each other.

Despite his shortness, Bahni made quite an impressive figure. There was a strange authority about him, an air which I could not analyse satisfactorily.

I wondered how I looked to him. I had not thought about my appearance since the day when, so long ago, Marie had told me that I was growing.

Seeing Bahni made me think. I rubbed my face, my hair, my hands felt each other. It all felt solid, healthy and well-fed.

I looked round the cavern. All those pathetic naked things occupying the place were potentially as I and Bahni. All that was needed was the nutriment and air that was denied them, and for the stumber to be taken away.

In a far corner, a massive Sleepee crouched, rocking to and fro, smiling inanely. It was Magnon. Poor Magnon!

'Well?' said Bahni.

'Sorry. I was thinking. Come and meet Gnofina, and then we'll go.'

Before we left, I quickly checked the cavern's equipment. It would save me time later, when I would have to return for maintenance on the others.

'All right?' asked Gnofina.

'Fine,' I said, waving the key in front of the door.

I looked at Bahni as we stood in the corridor when the door closed behind us. I thought the sound dramatic. For me, it marked the turning point in a life. But Bahni, whose life it was, seemed unmoved.

Gnofina cried a little.

We walked to the end of the corridor. 'Go on then,' I told Gnofina. She walked rapidly towards the next junction and turned it. Then she stopped, turned, and waved us on.

Her signal meant that there was no one in sight in the next corridor. We made our way rapidly towards her.

The system was not perfect, but at least it meant we had a chance of avoiding any head-on encounters between Bahni and a Texec.

For although his bearing had improved immensely since I brought him food from the cell, and had given him an air-enricher, there was still no doubting Bahni's status as a Sleepee. His pallor, his smallness, his weak eyes, his thin hair and poor teeth, his *smell* would betray him immediately, even to the most casual passer-by.

We were about half-way along the two hundred yards between junctions when it happened.

'Hi!'

Gnofina looked quickly in the direction of the man, gave us an 'all-clear' signal and disappeared.

'Don't look round,' I said. 'Don't run.'

Bahni and I started walking faster. I didn't think he would make it, but he was all right.

'Oi!'

The sound was nearer. The corridor echoed with the

sound of someone trotting – not running, just trotting fast enough to catch us up.

Without pausing we rounded the junction. Gnofina's 'all-clear' had meant that there was no one in the corridor when she turned the corner. But now, there just could be. You never knew, though. My feeling of relief was profound as I discovered that we had rounded into an *empty* corridor.

The man chasing us could no longer see us. We had a start.

'OK. Run,' I said to Bahni. He couldn't. I grabbed his hand and started sprinting down the corridor, towards Gnofina who was waiting at the next junction, looking anxious.

I remembered running along a corridor before. The corridor had been called a street and was wider, and I had been impeded by a lack of oxygen instead of by a companion whose legs were too feeble to perform adequately. And the fear had been internal rather than from without.

But the effect was much the same.

'Hey!'

This time I looked round. He was about a hundred yards away. He stopped and waved. 'Stop!' I put on as much of a spurt as I could, dragging the stumbling Bahni behind me. We made the final few yards to Gnofina.

'You two go ahead,' I said. 'It's the only way.'

Bahni began to protest, but Gnofina grabbed his hand and made off in the direction of the retribution corridor.

So much for our hopes of a clear run to the retribution cells.

Wearily, I waited for the man. I leaned against the wall and gulped down as much air as I could.

He was panting slightly as he came up to me.

'What's the matter with you?' he demanded roughly, emphasising the *you*. He was aggressive, but not totally hostile. I decided to play it stupid.

'Sorry,' I said.

86

'Sorry! he repeated. 'Anyone would think you were frightened of me.'

'Sorry,' I said.

'Oh well. We all make mistakes, I suppose. You dropped this.'

It was the little air enricher I used in the cavern.

'Oh. Thanks.' There was a silence. He looked at me. I felt that if I didn't say something he would suspect something. 'You see, my sister . . .' I pretended to look for words, hoping he would find them for me. He did.

He laughed, and came closer to me, and nudged me in the ribs.

'Oh, yeah?' he said. 'And your brother too, I suppose?'

I grinned and nodded. 'Yeah,' I said.

'You like it both ways, then?' I shrugged, grinned again, shuffled, tried to look embarrassed. I didn't know why I should be embarrased, but there was something in the tone of his voice that prompted me.

'Oh, well. I don't share your tastes, but I don't blame you. She looked all right, but I can't say I fancied the boy.' He laughed again.

'Why did you run away? Did you think I was his father – or were you just afraid of the competition. Eh?'

'Something like that,' I mumbled. My confusion was not assumed.

'Anyway, you've lost 'em both now. Never mind. Here's your air-enricher.'

'Thanks,' I said. 'Thanks very much.' And I turned to go.

I had gone only a few paces when he accosted me again.

'Wait a minute.' I stopped, sighing. It was the only way. 'Let's have another look at that enricher.'

I showed it to him.

'This is the sort they use in the caverns, isn't it?'

I nodded.

'No wonder you didn't want me to catch you,' he said. 'You're a dormy cavern-worker, aren't you?'

'Yes.'

'I see. One of the elite. One of our moral leaders, chosen

for the job for their rectitude and lousy purity. No venality – not with all that *flesh* to look after.'

I knew later what he meant. Had I known at the time I could have got rid of him; made some excuse, offered a bribe or a promise. I even considered violence, but it was obvious that he was more powerful than I.

He was still regarding me slyly.

I shrugged. 'So what do you want?' I asked.

He thought. 'A bit of privilege. A bit of extra comfort,' he said.

'You're a Texec – what more do you want?'

'Well. Like I said. A bit of privilege. A bit of extra comfort.'

If only I knew what he was talking about. 'If you could be more specific I might be able to help.'

'You'll have to help if you want to keep your job,' he said.

'Suppose I don't?'

'Well, you *must* do. All the cavern workers do. They've got the best jobs going.'

I hoped to be able to manipulate the conversation so that he would tell me something about himself without getting suspicious about me. I had stopped worrying about the other two. There was nothing I could do about them. They had either got to the safety of the cells or they hadn't.

'What do you do, then?' I asked.

He made a face. 'Reprocessor maintenance, mostly. Not nearly so good as cavern-working – or dream processing.' A light came into his eyes. 'Now there's a job for you!'

I snorted, pretended to be indifferent. 'No better than yours,' I said. 'Where do you live?'

'Two-Q-B.'

I made a guess, half remembering what Magnon had told me about Texec living quarters. 'You've got as much space as I have then,' I said.

He looked at me strangely. 'There's no need to be funny,' he said.

So I had been wrong. I decided to bluff it out. 'Surely you have?' I said.

'Well, of course I have,' he said. 'So has everybody else. That's not the point.'

I cursed myself for forgetting. Magnon had told me that all Texecs in Cubale had the same living space, the same amount of credit. They used something else to set them apart from each other.

Back in Lemington Texecs with different jobs had different standards of living. Here it was different. What was the difference?

I looked at the fellow, and caught him looking at me. But it was not at me, it was at what I wore.

'How about an outfit like this?' I asked, indicating Magnon's reduced one-piece.

'That's what I meant – didn't you understand?'

'Oh, well – in all the confusion . . .'

'Sure.'

It was a worth a try. The Texec was almost as big as Magnon, though much softer. If we went to Magnon's apartment together, it might be less risky than going by myself.

'O.K. Come on,' I said.

The walk to the apartment took about ten minutes. Feigning confidence I brandished the key at the door, which swung open. There was only one Texec within sight, and he didn't take much notice of us.

'Come in,' I said, as though I owned the place.

'Right.'

The door let into a vestibule, brilliantly lit, pale green and white. A stairway flanked each side by a banister of an ornate latticework curled upwards, while downstairs there were four doors, each with four panels, each of the panels bearing a different picture.

I longed to look at them, but I realized that any hesitation on my part would look odd, so I chose one of the doors at random, pushed it open and went into the room beyond.

I cursed. It was a bathroom.

'Excuse me,' I said, and shut the door, fastening it behind me with the manual lock.

Quickly I looked around the room and its plumbing.

Attached to the bath was a shower apparatus with a flexible hose.

I took the shower hose off a hook on the wall, brought it as close to the lavatory as I could, aimed it carefully, reached back to the bath, and turned on the water hard.

The effect was magnificent. A powerful jet of water hit the lavatory right where I was aiming, creating just the sound I was after.

After a short while I turned off the flow, and flushed the lavatory. Down tumbled three gallons – a Sleepee's ration for two days – and the act was over.

I walked out into the vestibule again. 'Sorry. I needed that,' I said.

The Texec was gone.

'You sure did,' he said.

Another door was open. I went through into the main room. He was standing at a slide library, idly projecting some images across forty feet on to the wall opposite.

'Nice collection,' he said.

'Make yourself at home,' I said.

'Yeah,' he said. 'How about that spare suit?'

'Well, I think I've got one to fit you . . .' I backed out of the room, closing the door behind me. I was doing better than I could have hoped for.

By going into the bathroom, I couldn't have gone through a wrong door that was more right. It had given me an excuse to stall, he had done some exploring on my behalf – and now there were only two more ground-flooor rooms to search.

I opened one of the doors. It let into a closet. I slammed it.

'You won't keep it in there, now will you?'

My heart sank. He had opened the door again and had come out to watch me.

I tried to laugh, shut the closet door and went quickly to the fourth door.

'Look, quit stalling will you? Just go up to your bedroom and get me the suit. Then I'll get out of here.'

He never knew how grateful I was. So Texecs kept their clothes in their bedrooms, and their bedrooms were up. It was something I had never known.

'All right, all right,' I said, and started climbing the stairs. He followed me.

As I climbed, I tried to put myself into Magnon's head. If this was my apartment, where would my bedroom be? I thought it would be above the biggest room on the ground floor, because that was where the biggest bedroom itself was likely to be.

So I chose the door that led into the room above the living room. Pushing it open I strolled in carelessly. It looked as though I had, for the first time, chosen right.

On the wall facing us was a series of narrow doors attached one to the other. In the centre of the room a huge bed, elsewhere some ornamented boxes, chairs, a washbasin.

But no clothes.

'Go on, then,' he said. 'Open up the wardrobe.'

'Er – go ahead, you do it. Help yourself,' I said.

It worked.

'OK,' he said, shrugging. 'It's your house.'

If only he'd known! The thought of the risks I was running made me feel suddenly weak at the knees.

Not only were my life or liberty at stake, but my whole design as well. We were so vulnerable!

'Wow!' said the Texec.

I looked at him. He was standing in front of the opened cupboards, all hung with a series of the sort of one-pieces I had always seen Magnon wear. At the centre of this array these reached from hook to ground an outfit in a deep and brilliant red.

All the clothes were huge. It was obvious that they were not mine. But my companion did not notice. He could not stop looking at the red one-piece.

I moved up behind him and closed all the doors but those

opening on to the compartment holding the red garment. He looked on it as though in a trance.

'It's yours,' I said. He looked at me quickly and back again. 'Mine?' he said. 'Oh, no. I couldn't. I wouldn't ever have let on about you, not really. You don't have to give me this. Anything would do. Not this. I couldn't.'

He seemed to be troubled by conscience. Or was it fear? I could not tell. I wished that he would go.

'Oh, take it and go,' I said.

'But it must have taken you years to get one of these . . . oh, all right,' he said. 'I'll try it on.' Quickly he pulled off his robe and pants, and eased himself into the one-piece.

'How do I look?'

'Great. I should take it home and show your friends.'

'But won't they mind . . . outside?'

'Who?'

'The other cavern workers.'

'Why should they?'

'Why should they?' he echoed my question. 'You give me the uniform of a Texec council master – of the caverns, mark you, of the elite – and then you ask me why your colleagues should object?'

He shrugged in sudden acquiescence.

'Oh well. If you say it's all right.'

'Surely,' I said. 'Well . . . that's it, then.'

'If you say so.'

I walked across to the door and opened it.

'I'd better be going,' he said.

'If you don't mind. I've rather a lot to do.'

'Indeed?'

He came over to me, looked puzzled for an instant, then smiled.

'You're a strange fellow,' he said. 'You're sure you want to give me the outfit?'

'Yes.'

'And they won't mind?'

'No!'

He hesitated and then, to my relief, made for the stairway.

'Er, so long.'

'So long,' I said, and waved as he let himself out of the front door below.

Although I should have been happy at his departure, when it came, I felt worried. Why had he been so hesitant over taking the one-piece? It was the one he wanted, wasn't it?

Magnon's apartment fronted on to a square. I watched the Texec in Magnon's red one-piece walk slowly across it.

Through the one-way transparent wall of the bedroom I saw another Texec wearing a black one-piece and skull cap come out of his door and go straight over to him.

They started talking, and then arguing. To my distress the Texec who had just left me pointed across the square towards the apartment, obviously telling the other where he had been.

I felt as though I should find a way of escape, but could not resist watching them.

The discussion had turned into an argument. They were gesticulating and shouting at one another. I wished that I could hear them.

Then the Texec in the black one-piece pulled out a device that had been lying within his collar. It was golden, cylindrical and about two inches in length. I saw that it was attached to a thin chain, and remembered that Magnon had worn a similar apparatus around his neck.

Black one-piece put the cylinder to his lips and appeared to blow. Immediately a thin high sound came into the room, and seconds later two or three more Texecs also wearing black came into the square and ran towards the couple.

Together they formed a semicircle about the Texec in red as he stood with his back against a wall. From time to time he looked towards the apartment as though he was expecting help from there – from me. I stayed put.

Then all discussion seemed to stop. The Texec in red made what appeared to be a final, despairing plea, which was answered by a peremptory gesture from one of the others. Then he began to fumble at the neck fastenings and parted the magnetic clips, one by one, until he was able to take the garment off.

There was a strange quality of dignity about him as he stood at bay in his underclothes, offering Magnon's one-piece to his persecutors. Another gesture from one of them and he removed the skull cap. Another short, threatening sign, and he began to fold the garment.

That done, he handed it to one of the company who looked at it, shook it loose, and threw it back at him.

Wearily, he started to fold it again. Then he handed it over again. This time the way he had folded the garment seemed to meet with approval, for it was not returned to him a second time.

The Texecs stood aside as though to let him go. He sprinted forward and tripped on an outstretched foot and fell.

The Texec who had first accosted my former companion jumped into the air, bringing his knees almost up to his chest and then straightened out his legs again to land his feet on the inert, half-clothed body.

Then his colleagues followed suit until the creature on the ground stopped trying to avoid them and lay quite still.

One of the Texecs stood back from the scene. He was holding Magnon's one-piece to him, and against his chest it resembled a great splash of fresh blood. He began to walk towards Magnon's apartment.

Two of the others took hold of their victim's legs and dragged him towards one of the doors on the other side of the square, opened it and pulled him inside. The rest dispersed.

I felt sick. The dead Texec had presented a threat to me, and I was the sworn enemy of his kind, yet I felt remorse. That I should feel this emotion in sending him to that encounter – however inadvertently – I found disturbing.

By now the red splash was very close. Soon he would be trying the door. Then he would knock. And then, if there

were no reply, he would go. He would either get assistance
to have the door opened, to see if there were anything wrong
in Magnon's apartment, or he would go away – and watch.

I could hear him try the door. Then he knocked on it.

He must not be allowed to escape now. If I let him go, I
would be trapped. Grabbing a tall statuette of some heavy
material as I left the room, I made my way to the stairs. I
hurried. Soon he would tire of knocking.

I ran to the door, reached for the handle with one hand
while the other held the statuette over my shoulder, ready
to strike.

'No!'

I turned quickly, terrified.

It was Gnofina.

She was standing at the fourth door, the one I had not
opened before, next to the closet. She made an undignified
figure, one that I would have found comical in other
circumstances: she was covered from head to feet in bits of
fluff and pieces of waste. The front of her tunic was
smeared with green nutriment of some sort.

'Come on,' she said. 'In here.'

I dropped the statuette and ran towards her. Outside,
the knocking stopped. She beckoned me into the room. I
looked quickly out of the wall and saw the Texec turn
away from the door.

'He'll be back soon,' she said. 'We've got to get out of
here.'

'How?'

She grinned.

'By the way I got in,' she said. 'Through the reprocessor
duct.'

All Texec apartments in Cubale were fitted with a chute
for surplus goods. At the bottom of the chute ran a belt
which took the goods to a reprocessor unit.

'Isn't that dangerous?'

'Very. But not so dangerous as this place. Do just what I
tell you. Down you go.'

My heart pounding, I climbed into the chute, let go, and lifted my arms above my head.

My feet hit the belt before my arms were free of the chute. I fell. Gnofina came after me and fell too. Her foot struck me in the face.

It was black down there. I tried to get up, but the tube was too narrow and I hit my head against the top as I tried to do so.

Gnofina shouted above the rumble of the belt.

'We'll be OK for a few minutes. Then we come to the junction where two more belts meet this one and discharge their load into the pulping unit. That's where you have to be careful.'

She wasn't joking.

She continued: 'When you get there you'll see some superstructure supporting the mechanism. Grab it and hold on. I'll overtake you there and lead you on to the next belt.'

Answering my unspoken question, she went on: 'You'll have to crawl fast to stay in one place there – you'll be heading against the direction of the belt. To get anywhere against the flow you'll have to really shift, believe me. OK?'

'How will I know when we get to the junction?'

'You'll see it,' she said, and switched on a flashlight.

'That's a relief.'

'Yeah. I'll have to hold this in my mouth, and I'll be coming right after you, so don't rely on it too much. I can't guarantee you a steady beam.'

She switched the flashlight off again, presumably to avoid any risk of dazzling me with it. The sensation of movement was not great as we made our way towards the reprocessor belt.

'Why are you doing all this for me?' I asked.

The rumble was growing louder.

She shouted something. It sounded like, 'Getting nearer.'

The flashlight beam went over me to light up the junction ahead. The metal web above and around it glimmered here and there in the light, and heaps of garbage shone palely as they came towards us from the approaching tunnels, to disappear into the mechanical maw below.

'Grab high!'

I heard her too late as I reached out, held desperately on to a strut. The belt skidded against my legs momentarily before I swung out over the void.

The top tooth of the primary pulper bit hard. As I twisted my foot out of its shoe I felt the rasp and sting of an edge against the skin.

Another fraction of a second, another fraction of an inch one way or the other and it would have pulled me down for eventual delivery to the organic wastes reprocessing unit.

A shower of garbage from the district waste chute immediately above spattered over my head and fell into the pulper and was gone.

I brought my knees up and found a foothold. I clung to the web desperately as Gnofina reached out and grabbed higher than I had, and trod on my shoulder as a step.

Then she was gone. I felt the blood dripping from my foot. The light flashed and bobbed as she made her way into the tunnel opposite. A twinge of cramp in my thigh terrified me as I followed, but it went as I scrambled after her.

She was not so much crawling as jumping, bringing her legs up and stretching them out again with as much force as she could. I could not keep up with her, and then I noticed her silhouetted arms stretched out sideways. To help her resist the flow of the belt, she was pressing against the sides of the tunnel. As soon as I had mastered the technique I found that progress was less difficult.

We bent and stretched our way up the tunnel for what seemed hours. The sweat poured into my eyes and made them sting. Piles of garbage accumulated themselves against us and we had to wriggle and buck to allow them through.

Gnofina dropped the flashlight and I halted, my forearms pressed against the sides of the tunnel. I watched the glow approach me and then dropped a hand to snatch it from the belt. I grabbed the flashlight, but as I did so, rolled on

97

to my back and was carried along on the belt before I could right myself. Then I had to make up the lost ground.

It was even more difficult than before with the torch in my mouth.

She was waiting for me, holding on to a protuberance in the wall, letting the belt run under her body, which rose and fell limply with the flow.

I gave her the flashlight, ran back with the belt and then came up to her again, as close as I could. I knew that I would be unable to go much further.

'I'm . . . almost . . . finished.' I could barely utter the words.

'Nearly there,' she shouted. 'Hang on. I'll send a rope.'

She gave the flashlight back to me and started crawling up the tunnel again. I took hold of the protuberance which she had used to anchor herself and shone the beam after her. The belt ran and scraped under me. Now I was static, its speed seemed much less than before, when I was fighting against it.

Gnofina's rump rose and fell as she slowly advanced up the tunnel; then, about thirty feet away, she stopped, gripping on to something on the top of the tunnel.

She twisted round and sat up, facing me. I could hear her shouting: '. . . Hold on . . . two minutes.'

Then her body disappeared into the top of the tunnel and, running backwards with her feet, straightened out so that she was visible only from the hips down. Her feet rose slowly as she pulled herself up and eventually they, too, disappeared.

For what seemed an age, nothing happened. Then a shaft of light struck down from the aperture into which Gnofina had gone, and then a line came down.

I shone the flashlight beam at it where it left the pool of light from above and watched its progress towards me. Slowly, incredibly slowly, it approached me. I gripped the flashlight between my teeth again and put out my free hand for the rope. I held it and twisted my hand so that the line encircled it several times.

I pulled as hard as I could on the line to test it and then let go of my anchor-hold above.

Again I was struggling to make headway along the tunnel. But this time with a line to give me courage and assist my progress. I heaved against it and moved forward. Soon the line and I established a working relationship. I found that within seconds of my having moved forward it would become tight again so that I did not have to renew my grip.

So we eased ourselves forward, my rope and I. Everything had become unreal. The rumble of the moving belt had become a roar. The little piles of garbage became great unfriendly monsters. I could no longer tell top from bottom, right from left. Objects caught in the beam of my flashlight began to grow eyes.

The only real thing in my universe was the line which was pulling me to safety, away for ever from the threat of mastication by the pulper.

Something was different in this universe. There was a subtle physical change. I found that I was unable to make as much headway as before. What was stopping me?

I shook my head hard, trying to make it think. Then I noticed that the hand holding the line was no longer immediately in front of me, but was pointing upwards.

The line itself was stretching upwards at a steep angle. I peered up and ahead, and saw that the line went into the tunnel roof. I was there! Nearly. I heard Gnofina's voice, but could not make out the words.

Painfully and slowly I got myself under the hole and twisted myself upwards through the hole, up the chute, and found my feet giving way underneath me. I ran backwards against the belt as Gnofina had done and straightened up.

Above me there was light, and a handhold. Inch by inch I scrabbled up the tube. First I could crook my wrists over the inlet, then, hours later it seemed, my elbows, then my armpits were over the top. The combination of the brilliant light and the sweat pouring into my eyes blinded

99

me. Where was Gnofina, though? She could have helped me out of this.

Slowly I emerged. I heaved myself out of the garbage tube until I could bend my waist. I leaned forward until I could touch the floor with my hands. Then my rump and legs wriggled out. I fell into a heap on the floor and lay there panting, almost paralysed with exhaustion.

Eventually I was able to look around the room. I did so several times before convincing myself that I was not mistaken.

I was quite alone.

9

So far as I could tell, the room was exactly similar to its counterpart in Magnon's apartment.

It might have been the same place except for the line coming from the garbage chute, running along the floor and being tied to a hook on the wall, low down.

Not that I particularly cared about my surroundings. I didn't really care about anything. All I wanted to do was to switch off, to stop thinking, to sleep.

I realized then that I was filthy. Looking down, I saw that my black one-piece was grey and sticky where waste nutriment had been smeared on it by the belt. Lumps of fluff and pieces of paper hung from me in festoons, and my face and hands were ingrained with surplus organic matter. My foot was still bleeding. I trailed red footmarks behind me. It stung badly, but it could have been a lot worse.

Suddenly a desire to clean myself up became overwhelming. I knew where the downstairs bathroom was, and limped towards it. It was empty. It had never occurred to me that it should be otherwise. I must have been in some sort of dream. I was in a Texec's house, a fugitive, uninvited. Had the occupants discovered me there that would have been the end of everything. And I no longer had to think of myself, but for Bahni, too. And maybe for Gnofina as well.

And yet I took no precautions.

I removed the one-piece, threw it into the basin, and poured hot water on to it. The dirt rolled out. I let out the water, pulled the garment out of the basin, shook out the remaining dirt, and hung it over a chair. Then I did the same with my underclothes before getting under the shower.

Standing there, luxuriating in the hot needles that soaked away the filth and fatigue of the past hour, I suddenly froze and switched off the flow.

The sound of water falling down the wastepipe continued. Someone was using the bathroom above.

But the voices I had heard, or thought I had heard, were silent now.

Quickly and quietly I dressed myself. The water from my wet body rapidly transferred itself through the coverings to the outside where it stood for an instant in beads, like sweat, and then rolled off.

Clean, dry, refreshed and trembling I listened again but could still hear nothing. I felt that it was worse than useless to stay where I was, so gingerly opened the bathroom door and looked out.

There was no one within sight so I went to the door to the outside and looked outside. That was no good. The corridor was busy, filled with Texecs.

The only thing to do was to wait. Magnon had told me that most Texecs kept a spare room in the upstairs part of their apartments. It was a room they hardly ever used, for few had guests, and I figured that if my memory was right, that would be the safest place for me. I could wait in there for a while and try my luck later on. If the occupants returned, then I would remain in their empty room, trust that they would not come into it, and try to escape when the apartment was quiet again.

I ran up the stairs as fast as my foot would allow me, and paused at the top. I remember that Magnon's bedroom door had been to the left, and that the bathroom was immediately on top of the one below. That left a choice of two doors. I decided to choose the one on the right, which led to the room immediately above the one I had first entered. Cautiously I pushed it open.

For an instant I stood there, immobilised. A couple were together naked on the bed.

Before I backed out, she saw me, and winked.

The sense of shock gave way to one of relief as I stood outside on the landing.

We were safe after all, or comparatively so. Presumably the Texec with Gnofina was friendly, at least towards her, and yet . . .

In her wink was a greeting. But a warning too. Danger was not imminent but it was there, somewhere in the apartment, or in our circumstances. It had seemed also that she wanted me to leave the room, not to announce myself. Well, fair enough. She had said that Texecs usually do these things in private.

But why had she gone to bed with him there and then? Surely her inclination should have been to see me safely out of the tunnel first and then gone ahead? She had told me that she was a whore, and liked sex too much, but this behaviour was nevertheless odd.

I went downstairs and got myself a meal. Half way through I got up, put a chair against the door just in case. And I was glad later that I had, for he tried the door on his way out.

It gave a little, and then stuck, and I heard her say: 'No, not that one,' or something like that. There was an urgency in her voice which made me think that perhaps it was he, after all, who was the source of danger.

They made farewell noises, and then the front door opened and closed. I saw him start to walk away. He was a big, fair man, and wore the loose tunic of someone in the thinking trades – a dream processor, perhaps, or an administrator of some sort.

Then I went to the door and took away the chair.

She came in. She looked at me and her eyes filled with tears. Sobbing, she put her arms around me and clung to me. I supported her as she swayed in my arms.

Without saying anything she let go and took my hand, and led me out of the room and up the stairs. We went into a different room and got on to the bed there, where first she made love to me and then I to her.

'How was Bahni? Did you leave him in the cell?' I asked afterwards.

She seemed not to hear me.

'I had to do it,' she said. 'He would have betrayed us otherwise. He knew me, you see. And he knew I shouldn't be here, but in the cells. So I pretended that I had got out for just a short while, on leave. But he said he would tell the council unless I went to bed with him. I didn't want to, and I wouldn't have, but for you. So I took a shower while he waited for me.' She laughed, a little bitterly. 'Can't think why he wanted me. I was all covered in bits of garbage. I suppose he thought I had escaped from the cells that way. I didn't want to. I did it for you. I'm sorry, I'm sorry . . .'

'Sorry?' I said. 'But that's ridiculous. It's I who should be sorry.'

Somehow, it was the wrong answer. I tried again.

'Well, I thought it was a bit irresponsible of you at first,' I said. 'But I now see that it was the best thing you could do. I'm really grateful. I'll never be able to pay you back. Never.'

But that was the wrong answer too. She gave a sort of strangled groan and got off the bed. Then she picked up a bottle and threw it at the mirror. They both smashed, and broken glass littered the floor.

'Hey!' I said.

But she ran out of the room and slammed the door.

A minute or two later, I heard the sound of running water.

She was taking another shower. I slept.

Later, I tried again. 'How about Bahni?' I asked. She said: 'He's O.K. I left him in my cell. He should be safe. Hungry, but safe.'

'That's good. We can't risk losing him.' I looked at her. 'How come you were on to me so quickly?' I asked.

'Oh, that.' She smiled. 'Well, when we left you, we raced to the cells – I had to drag poor little Bahni all the way – and then I ran back. You must have hung around for some time talking,' – I nodded – 'because I was just in time to see you at the other end of the corridor. I followed you as far as that apartment, Magnon's I presume?' Again I nodded. 'So then I came back here.'

She smiled, and then went on: 'This is my apartment, you see, and I used to live here even when I was a child with my parents. We used to run away down into the garbage tunnels sometimes – lots of the kids did it, until one got killed and we were all stopped – so I got to know the area pretty well, under the ground as well as above it.'

'Lucky for me you did.'

'Yes,' she said. 'It was. And lucky Magnon's apartment is so near.' She pointed out of the wall.

'You mean that one with the people in front?'

'That's the one.'

I had had no idea that it was so close. There it was; not more than 250 yards down the other side of the square was Magnon's residence. The door was open, and Texecs were bustling in and around it continually.

'They know something's up.'

She nodded. 'Yes. But if I know my people, the excitement will soon wear off, and they'll soon shelve the problem for tomorrow.'

'It will get quieter, then?'

'I imagine so.'

'Then wouldn't it be better for us to go now? If they are

104

all preoccupied with the mystery of Magnon's apartment, then they won't notice us, surely?'

'I think you're wrong. They'll be more on their guard. More likely to notice something or someone unusual. We'd do better to wait.'

'O.K. You know best.'

But I found waiting hard. As the hours went past I became increasingly preoccupied by the thought of Bahni alone in the cell. He would be worried and anxious, and there was no knowing what he might do if troubled badly by the symptoms of stumber withdrawal. Nor would he be able to feed himself, not knowing how to operate the nutriment dispenser.

Eventually I could stand it no longer.

'Look,' I said. 'If we wait here any longer we're going to start running more risks than if we leave now. Let's get back to the cells straight away.'

Gnofina shrugged assent.

'You go first. I'll trail you.' I said.

Silently she got off the seat and made her way to the door. Pausing for an instant to look outside, she opened it and went through.

I counted slowly up to sixty and followed her.

When I got into the corridor I could see her at the junction, just turning off into the passage that led back to the cells.

During my walk along the corridors to the cells I felt as frightened as I was in the garbage tunnel. Then, things had seemed almost hopeless and there was little left to lose. But now: we had beaten the system, we had kept ourselves and our project a secret, we had succeeded in building up a substantial and complicated edifice of deception, and yet still a simple accident could bring it tumbling down.

But my fears were misplaced: the journey back to the cells was uneventful. From time to time I saw Gnofina walking steadily ahead; not once did she look back to see if I were following. Frequently I looked over my shoulder to see if there were anyone behind, following me.

Seldom can a prisoner have been so pleased to see his jail as I was when I entered the retribution corridor. I could not prevent myself from running the final few yards, despite the pain in my foot.

I pushed on the door, which was unfastened, went through, turned round, slammed it and fastened my makeshift interior bolts.

'That's right, my little Sleepee. Make sure you're safe and sound,' said Magnon.

I held on to the door to steady myself and remained thus for some time before turning to face him.

Anyone else his size would have looked ridiculous in the clothes I had left behind in the cavern. But he was dignified – and menacing.

He seemed huger than ever. I ran across and punched him in the belly. It was like hitting a wall.

Magnon laughed and seized my fist, squeezing the fingers together so that it felt as though they were being pulped and compressed into a ball.

Then he twisted my arm and pushed me away. I staggered backwards across the cell again until my back struck the door. My head jerked up and struck the door and I blacked out momentarily. I felt myself falling to the floor. I lay there, waiting for the next blow.

But none came. Instead I felt hands helping me sit up. I rolled over on to my hands and knees, then knelt, then stood. Quickly I sat down again on the bed.

'I'm sorry,' said Magnon. 'I was too rough.'

'Yes, you were,' said Gnofina. 'You forget he's smaller than you.' She was sitting beside me.

'How are you?' It was Bahni, talking to me.

'How are *you*?' I said. My eyes had difficulty in focusing, but I could just about make him out. He shrugged. 'I'm fine now, although I was very scared at first. But when Magnon came along and looked after me, told me everything would be all right, showed me how to operate the nutriment dispenser, explained what this place was . . .'

'Stop. *Stop.*' I could hear myself screaming. The lights before my eyes fused and became one. Odd flesh-coloured globes swam into my vision and out again. Every so often an eye or a pair of eyes would look into mine and then merge once more with the walls around me.

I heard voices coming from another existence. They murmured words like 'hysteria,' and 'exhaustion,' and 'rest'. Some of them belonged to males, other to females. Once I was raised up and a liquid was passed between my lips. It left behind a thin trail of warmth in my gullet.

The flesh and bright lights and blues and yellows before me diminished into a mist and became as one; the voices, once shrill, became soothing and descended into a susurration which lulled me into oblivion.

I awoke to a feeling of well-being. There was a bustling sound in the cell as though its occupants were many and busy. I tried to look around me to see where the sounds were coming from but it was too much effort.

I closed my eyes again and my imagination roamed behind the thin red veil of their lids.

Idly I pondered upon the cause of so much business: who were the people I could hear?

Perhaps I was in a Texec hospital . . . no, I was still in the cell; I could tell that I was still lying on the bed I knew so well.

Perhaps we had been discovered, and I was being exhibited to passers-by as a curio. Again this seemed unlikely. They would not allow me to lie thus at peace.

No matter. I would learn, soon enough. My thoughts drifted away and my consciousness with them. Once more I drifted into sleep, and dreamed of the place I used to dream of under stumber, in the Lemington dormys.

But back there I *knew* in dreamstate that this place was real, and in wakestate, that it was not.

This time, I did not know whether it was real or unreal. But I knew that the existence of such a place was possible.

As wakefulness returned to me I felt the tears running down my face.

'He's coming to,' said Gnofina. 'Look.'

'Why, so he is.' The voice was Magnon's. But it no longer frightened me.

'Hello,' I said, and opened my eyes.

From where I lay I could see Gnofina and Magnon, and beyond them there was the cell, and beyond that a large room, painted white.

I looked to my right and saw the hole in the wall made by Gnofina when she wanted to make her way to my cell. And in the wall beyond my feet was another, **much larger** hole.

'What's down there?' I asked.

'Used to be the guards' quarters,' said Magnon. 'I decided we needed the space, so I knocked a hole through and there it was.'

'Needed the space?' I said. 'But what for. Who for . . . why?'

'Before you start talking, let's make you more comfortable and get you some nutriment,' said Gnofina. 'After all, you've been asleep for three days.'

'Three days?' Again I tried to sit up. Again the hands restrained me.

'And you, Magnon,' I said. 'I thought you were going to kill me.'

'That was before,' he said.

'And now you're no longer my enemy?'

'I'd like to be your ally,' he said. 'That time in the cavern taught me a lot. Made me think.'

'Despite the stumber?'

'Because of it. I felt myself enjoying it and all it brought. Then a sense of self-disgust made me fight it, and I knew what you had been through. It was tough, but I always thought to myself that if you could do it, I could. And because of your example, I did.'

'But I can't see why that puts you on my side. After all, it was I who put you in that position in the first place.'

108

He laughed. 'Yes, outwitted by a Sleepee! That taught me a lot. I can see now – after a lifetime of assuming otherwise – that the Sleepee is inferior to the Texec simply because the Texec makes him so. Give him the same environment as the Texec – and there's no difference. That's wrong. And if you want to change the life of the people, then I'm with you.'

I felt elated. If I could bring someone like Magnon to my side, then surely it was not impossible to convert an entire habitat?

Not knowing then what I know now, I held out my hand to him.

'By the way, how did you get out?' I asked.

He smiled as he grasped my hand. 'Spare key, of course. I didn't tell you everything. Not quite.'

I saw Gnofina. She was quite still, as though she had been standing there some time. She walked towards me.

'People?' said Gnofina.

She sat down on the bedside and began to spoon nutriment into my mouth. I tried to sit up, but she would have none of it, and with a sense of relief that I tried not to show, I leaned back again.

'People,' said Magnon. 'People are Texecs *and* Sleepees. They are humanity.'

'Um,' she said. 'Humanity. You mean human beings? I've heard of them. That's what we came from, isn't it?'

'That's what we still *are*,' said Magnon. 'And so are the Sleepees, too.'

'Are they really?' she said.

I pushed away the spoon. 'If you didnt believe that, why did you help me?'

'I'd do anything for you, you know that,' she said, thrusting the spoon between my lips.

'Yes, but why?' said Magnon.

'Oh, well – he's special,' she said, smiling.

'But if he's special, you can't think of yourself as superior to him,' said Magnon.

'I don't,' she said.

109

'But he's a Sleepee,' he said.

'Well, not really. I mean . . . he can do it, and Sleepees can't as a rule, can they?'

'That's just my point,' said Magnon. 'They can't because we Texecs feed them with drugs that prevent them. Is that right?'

She said: 'No, I suppose it isn't.'

'You *suppose* it isn't?' I pushed away her arm. 'Either it is or it isn't. There's nothing to suppose. Either you agree – and you're with us, or you don't, and you're not with us.'

My head throbbed. I heard her sobbing.

Magnon was comforting her. The carton of nutriment lay where it fell.

She must have left. There was no more talk for a while.

Later Magnon bent down to pick up the carton, offered it to me. Silently I waved it away.

'She's done more for you than anyone,' he said.

'But I was right,' I said.

For a moment he looked into the carton, as though hoping to find the right answer in the green and pink of its contents.

'People are going to take a lot of persuading,' he said.

But Gnofina and I made it up. As I regained strength, I learned what Magnon, with Bahni helping him, had been doing.

I had been right when I first came out of my coma to think that the cells were busier than usual. They were now occupied by an extra five Sleepees and two Texecs.

The latter people were young – students – who, being of an adventurous disposition and well known to Magnon, had been invited to join our enterprise. They were not committed to us as a group, but were loyal to Magnon.

Magnon had smuggled the Sleepees out of one of his caverns in a trolley used for carrying heavy equipment around Cubale.

Wryly I compared the ease with which he had carried

out the transfer of five Sleepees from cavern to cell with the way I had transferred Bahni.

But I had been the pioneer. I had been the first, and anyway I did not have the facilities available to a Texec. And Magnon told me that all he had done was as a result of what I had done. My small action, he said, had been the first link in a chain of actions that would alter the shape of existence.

Day after day we would talk. My cell became a centre for debate. Nearly always I was at the centre of discussion, and almost as frequently Magnon and Bahni were there, at least to begin with.

All I did, it seemed to me, was to initiate talk and reply to questions. Questions from young, eager Texecs, happy at the prospect of change – any change; questions from their elders (although few), liberal-minded and discreet guests, selected with care by Magnon; questions from Sleepees, still dull-eyed from the effects of stumber but filled with a ruthless desire to shake off those effects.

It was all stimulating and encouraging. Gnofina, oddly, became as skilled at debate as I, and led many a discussion when I was too tired, or when my voice was giving out.

But if I was providing the theories of revolution, Magnon was laying down its practical foundations.

Being himself at the centre of the Cubale establishment, he was able to visualise the best methods of deceiving it, and of manipulating it.

He fed the service programmes with false data so that we could come by any sort of supply without unbalancing the register of consumption. (For instance in the retribution cells we had ninety per cent of the region's supplementary inhalers: when the time came this could be a crucial factor in deciding the issue.)

He also altered the servicing frequency factor in the programme relating to the trolleys, arranging matters so that the repair shops would constantly be behind schedule. Major repairs could therefore no longer be dealt with at once, but would pile up in a backlog – so that when the time came, the Texecs would be short of trolleys and unable to travel as swiftly from one sector to another as they would wish.

But Magnon made quite sure that we would have sufficient trolleys.

Broadly our plan was to wean a number of Sleepees from stumber, and then to teach them how to administer a cavern. When they were fully trained, they would return to the caverns and, in turn, select other Sleepees for training.

They would be able to operate from within the caverns when necessary, making them habitable by using a preparation which neutralised the stumber contained in the nutriment and drinking fluids.

The Sleepees who were trained in the caverns would, it was hoped, train others, and the others, others, until eventually there would be a sufficient number of stumber-free Sleepees to talk on terms of equality with the Texecs. Or so we hoped.

One of the biggest problems later on would be the transfer of trained Sleepees to other caverns so that they could spread the seeds of revolution, but Magnon promised to have the problem solved within time.

I still do not know how Magnon managed to adjust the nutriment and atmosphere distribution figures so that Cubale's central administration never once suspected (so far as I know) that there were at one stage ten times as many occupants of the retribution cells as there were official prisoners: that the number of Sleepees in any number of caverns altered by as many as three more or less from one day to the next; that a number of cavern administrators disappeared mysteriously to be replaced instantly by people no one recognized.

The undercurrent of subversive activity was terrific, but very little showed on the surface. And the Texecs of Cubale, soporific in the luxury of their homes, absorbed in the pursuit of pleasure, inclined out of laziness to dismiss the tiny signs of disorder that, despite all precautions, manifested themselves, remained oblivious.

For six months we worked. The response from the Sleepees to our call was more eager than we had dreamed possible. In some of the caverns, almost half the occupants were weaned from stumber; in very few were there fewer than a quarter ready to join the revolt.

Magnon, meanwhile, had returned to Texec society, apparently normal, explaining that his absence had been caused by a sudden illness, and he had preferred to recover privately. This was accepted for he was a respected figure and well liked.

Even if I hadn't known that the revolution had started, I would have been able to tell by the sudden diminution of the proportion of oxygen in the atmosphere as hundreds of Sleepee leaders opened the doors of their caverns.

Their inferior breathing mixture mingled with the top-grade air of the public places, and thousands of Sleepee lungs breathed, for the first time in years, the concentration of oxygen that they had been designed for.

The morning of the revolution wore on, and the atmosphere grew thinner and fouler as, stimulated by the oxygen-rich atmosphere they breathed, the Sleepees became more active.

Later in the day Magnon came to the cell. Gravely he kissed Gnofina, and shook my hand. His colour was high and he breathed rapidly. I gave him an inhaler.

'Don't worry,' I said. 'You'll soon get used to the atmosphere. You, too, Gnofina.'

Poor as the air was, it was still better than what I had had to breathe at times in the past.

'Oh yes,' said Magnon. 'I got used to it in the cavern. But then I wasn't doing much.'

We looked at one another. None of us was going to be able to do much in Cubale for some time now.

'How did it go?' I asked.

'Perfectly,' said Magnon. 'There's nothing the Texecs

will be able to do about it. All the cavern doors are open and half the Sleepees are now out exploring their habitat, using up the Texecs' atmosphere, plundering his nutriment reserves in the public eating-places, overloading his reprocessing units. So much for our plans – that's all we had to do, just open the doors. The Texec is now harmless to us. Negotiation is obsolete, unnecessary. They, as well as the Sleepees, will soon want someone to organize them. And *they* will come to *us*!'

We all laughed, but we didn't really think that it was funny.

By instigating the revolution we had offered freedom to the Sleepees, and a challenge to the Texec supremacy. But we were also presenting many with death.

It was inevitable that with the entire population of Cubale sharing the resources on an equal basis, that there would be insufficient to go round. Many would become weak in the thin atmosphere and would die sooner than they might have done, others could starve.

The large number of cadavers would also throw the reprocessing units out of balance. There would be at first an insufficiency and then a surplus of waste.

But after all that, when the living unit that was Cubale had readjusted itself, there would be a surplus of reprocessed goods too – nutriment, clothing, water, power, would be there in abundance.

Then the people, fewer in number, could thrive upon the plenitude offered by Cubale. They could prosper and progress in equality. They, the fittest who had survived, could establish a society which would be envied and eventually emulated by all the other habitats.

10

'I don't think they'd mind back in Lemington,' I told Magnon one evening.

There was a lack of nutriment and the atmosphere was deteriorating. We moved sluggishly. Our thoughts were clear, but we had difficulty in expressing them. Magnon made no reply, but I could see that he was listening.

'I mean, they were much more liberal to the Sleepees to start with than your people. There the Texecs took less of the habitat's resources and gave the Sleepees more – not that the Sleepees were any happier as a result, but that's beside the point.'

Bahni, too, was looking interested.

I went on: 'And look at me. They took me, a Sleepee, and made me almost one of them. That would never have happened here, would it? They don't consider the difference between the Sleepee and the Texec to be as great as they do – did – here.'

'Don't fool yourself, brother,' said Magnon, smiling. 'They were just as concerned about being the élite as we ever were. It was just that they were more subtle in some ways, more stupid in others. And they were just as ruthless. You say they almost made you one of them? Don't make me laugh.'

He coughed, took three or four deep breaths and continued: 'They just wanted to get you to work for them. They taught you exactly what they thought you ought to know and no more, so that you, and others like you, could do all their work for them without getting their privileges. You say that would never have happened here. You're quite right. That's because the Texecs here knew that it would never work – as it didn't with you in Lemington.'

'But it did work,' I said. 'I learned very quickly.'

He waved me down. 'It didn't work from their point of view. As soon as they took you off stumber, you got interested in sex. You didn't know it, but you were. Then you developed a curiosity of your own. That's why you went to the "house of the little people" as you called it. Little people nothing. They were new Texecs – children. Only the Texecs breed, and not very fast at that for all their primary activity in the reproduction process, and they didn't want you even to know about children. They stopped the Sleepees having children at about the time you were born. That's why you were attacked in that house – so that you wouldn't find out their one great secret. And as soon as you showed signs that you were getting interested in that girl . . .'

'Marie,' I said.

'That's right, Marie – then they shipped you off here. They didn't mind the idea of getting a few Sleepees doing their work for them, but if this meant that the Sleepees became sexually aware again, the Lemington Texecs weren't interested any more.'

A lot of things I hadn't understood before were beginning to fall into place. But not everything.

'So their experiment failed, and they wanted to get rid of me.'

Magnon nodded.

'But there were many simpler ways of disposing of me. And they went to great lengths to deceive me. Why did they send me down here, when one of their retribution cells would have done just as well? Or a good strong shot of stumber would have done the trick, come to that.'

'They couldn't be sure about the stumber. Look at me – I shook it off quickly. You might have made trouble. You had before, after all. And it so happened, too, that you made a useful exchange for someone we wanted to send up there. And as for the rest of it – well, I guess someone was looking after you.'

That puzzled me.

'Well, they wanted you to be let down gently, without suspecting what was happening. Someone didn't want you hurt. That was the impression I got when I received my instructions about you. "Just make him a proper Sleepee again," I was told. "But so he doesn't realize it".'

I laughed. It was so ridiculous. 'That would have been impossible,' I said. 'I was terrified from the moment I got here. I knew something was up. And you knew I knew.'

'Nevertheless, someone was trying to be kind,' said Magnon. 'I expect it was that girl, Marie. You have a lot to thank her for.'

A sudden noise in the corner reminded me Gnofina was still with us. She got up and walked over to Magnon. She drew breath through an inhaler. 'You do talk a lot of nonsense. How do you know someone -- this Marie – was trying to be kind. You've no proof of any kind. It isn't even a good guess. What a stupid thing to say!'

She was furious. I was astonished. Magnon was amused.

'Maybe you're right,' he said. 'Maybe you're right, Gnofina. Could be it wasn't her at all.' Then he spoke to me: 'Maybe it was one of the men, hey, Phillips?'

'Perhaps,' I said, still mystified. 'Could have been Antonio, I suppose. He was always very friendly.'

'Of course. Antonio. How foolish of me, Gnofina. It was Antonio. Is that better?'

'Oh, perhaps you're right,' said Gnofina. 'Sorry I lost my temper.'

'That's OK,' said Magnon. 'We're all a little nervous. It's the atmosphere.'

Gnofina kept out of our way for the rest of the evening. Once or twice I asked if there was anything wrong, but this seemed to make her angry so eventually I gave up.

Besides it was getting difficult to concentrate on anything but the stench that was hanging over the cells. It seemed to penetrate everything – even the filter on the inhalers.

'Don't worry,' said Magnon. 'In a few days the system will have adjusted itself and we'll be breathing a good, wholesome atmosphere again.'

Later Gnofina said: 'I don't know how you could live through it . . . was the air in the caverns always like this?'

'No,' I said. 'It was never like this. But if it doesn't get better soon,' I whispered, 'we'll all choke.'

'Yes,' croaked Magnon and nodded as though to himself.

Gradually the process of living in Cubale slowed down. The automatic services continued to function but the beings for whom they functioned lay torpid in the foul and meagre atmosphere given out by the overworked conditioners.

After a few days, Magnon, Bahni and I decided that it would be safe to leave the cells and walk the corridors of Cubale. Doubtless many would blame us for their plight – and rightly – but without a good supply of oxygen to sustain their anger, they would be unlikely to give it effective expression.

Each equipped with a spare bottle of oxygen, we left the cells and soon arrived at the Texecs' residential zone in the centre of Cubale.

The zone, which I remembered as so well-ordered, presented a sorry sight. As he looked upon it, Magnon groaned. I laughed. We looked at one another wryly. The differences between us were still to be eliminated.

Yet I could see his point of view. The neat rows of apartments, the pleasantly decorated corridors and squares had had some aesthetic appeal – if only to the few who could appreciate it.

In the disorder – the doors unclosed, the litter-strewn surfaces, the bodies sprawled across the walkways – I saw the downfall of Texec supremacy.

If chaos now reigned in the place of order, at least it reigned impartially. If discomfort was the lot of one, it was the lot of all; and if the Sleepee had not yet come up to the level of the Texec, then the Texec had gone down to the level of the Sleepee.

But was that last true? I wondered! Was a Texec deprived of privilege not still better off than a Sleepee deprived of stumber? Or were they on a par in their misery?

It was a nice philosophical point which I chose not to pursue too far as we made our way along the main thoroughfare.

Most of the people there gazed at us dully, without interest. 'Oxygen deprival,' I said, observing their sluggishness and their colour. Magnon nodded. 'Depressing, isn't it?' he said. 'Nonsense,' said Bahni. 'This is only the first stage.'

Then, faint but unmistakeable, the smell which had plagued us in the cells returned.

We looked at each other in surmise. 'How strange,' said Bahni. 'I hadn't noticed that it had gone.'

'Neither had I,' said Magnon. 'But it's stronger than ever now.'

We stopped. I felt nauseated. Then it passed. I looked at Magnon, who was swallowing hard.

We advanced again, and the smell grew stronger.

Reluctant to breathe, our lungs and larynxes wheezed and rattled as the foulness was sucked into them and expelled again.

The inhalers helped, but did not succeed in making breathing pleasant. They made breathing preferable to suffocation, but only just. I felt that without the inhaler I would rather have died than continue to breathe.

Reeling forward, stomachs heaving, lungs panting in shallow bursts, we continued our tour of inspection, simply because the mental effort of placing one foot in front of the other meant that our minds were not concentrated exclusively upon the odour.

Then, suddenly, it began to clear again. Gingerly at first, then with increasing confidence, one by one we removed the inhalers and sniffed.

Bahni said: 'It reminds me of something, but I don't

know what. It sort of conjures up a half-memory, but a very vivid one.'

'Yes, you're right . . .' I recalled a scene in which shapes loomed and receded in the darkness, in which there was a wailing, and things towered above me. I knew what Bahni meant. It was vivid all right, but indistinct, as though I were looking at the scene through imperfect and alien eyes.

'There's a rational explanation for it, bound to be,' said Magnon. 'We knew that things would be thrown off balance for a while. After all, the complex of Cubale is a very delicate mechanism, adaptable up to a point, and able to maintain its equilibrium through changing conditions. But now conditions have changed too much for the balancing mechanism to cope. So things go wrong. I expect the smell is coming from an overworked air-conditioner. The conditioner's computer will be aware of the fault, and will attempt to rectify it. Alternatively, it will call in human assistance, and a maintenance man will correct it. But these things will take time. We knew they would. We must wait.'

Magnon was, we felt, absolutely right.

We had thrown the untrammelled demands of an entire population, hitherto tightly controlled, against a habitat system which though vast and ingenious had an ultimately limited capacity.

Already the atmosphere had declined in quality; soon the sewage and garbage reprocessors would show signs of excessive load. The power supply would doubtless also begin to fall short of the demands made upon it.

But eventually, we had reasoned, demand would drop to meet supply. There would be fewer people making more modest demands, and they would be demanding on terms of equality and merit; a new, equitable society would be forged, and this habitat, and eventually perhaps others, too, would benefit.

But in the meantime . . .

'Let's go back,' said Magnon. 'We've seen enough.'

Bahni and I agreed, and we took a circuitous route

towards the cells, not wishing to go over the same ground twice.

After about fifteen minutes' brisk walking, we came close to the cells. We started to slow down. Then we halted.

'That conditioner of yours is playing up again,' said Bahni.

Magnon's face was a mask of distaste. 'What a welcome,' he said. 'I wanted to do some work, and I'll never be able to concentrate until it goes off.'

'Why don't you investigate the machines yourself?' I asked him.

'Not my job,' he said. 'I'm a cavern supervisor, not a maintenance engineer.'

Bahni and I looked at one another. Magnon had been working too hard.

We got to my old cell and pushed our way in. Inhalers clasped firmly to our faces, we sat.

Gnofina was lying on the bed. She was very pale. 'You're back,' she said. 'I thought I'd go mad. Every time I breathe it's like excrement. We'll never live through it. Never.'

Tears rolled down the sides of her face.

'We all know it's bad,' I said. 'But at least it comes and goes. It isn't with us all the time.'

Slowly her head turned round and she looked at me. 'Comes and goes?' she asked. 'I don't understand.'

'Well, like I said . . . shortly after we left it went. Then later it came back, and went again . . .'

But she was standing, unsteady on her feet. She lurched towards the door, opened it and went outside. Slowly she walked up the corridor away from the cells.

'I'll go with her,' I said.

I caught her up. 'Where are you going?' She did not reply. We kept walking for a while. Gradually the smell began to fade. 'There, what did I tell you?' Again she made no reply. After a few more yards she stopped.

We breathed in gratefully through our inhalers. 'It's gone,' I said. 'The atmosphere's no worse now than it was in the caverns.'

'It hasn't gone, she said.

'What?'

'The smell, of course.' There was a flicker of anger in her exhaustion. 'It hasn't gone at all. You go back to the cell. Go on.'

I walked away. She was right. As I approached the cells, the odour returned. I stopped, sniffed, repressed a desire to vomit, swallowed and went back to her.

'You're right,' I said. 'It's local and permanent, not general and intermittent. The smell's confined to certain areas. Maybe its just the occasional outlet, rather than the system. Let's go and tell Magnon.'

'You go ahead. I'll stay here. Don't forget, I've had it all day,' said Gnofina.

I couldn't blame her. Bracing myself for the malodorous onslaught, I made my way back to the cells again.

At first Magnon appeared disbelieving, until I offered to prove that the smell was local by carrying him out of the locality.

'No, no, I believe you,' he said. 'It's just that I can't see how it's happening. Maybe I *could* take a look.'

'You're the only one. And it doesn't really matter any more if it isn't your job, does it?' I asked.

'Suppose not.'

But the local outlet for the cells revealed nothing. Indeed, the atmosphere was sweeter in its proximity than anywhere else within a radius of 100 yards.

'It's worst just here,' said Bahni. He was standing by a cell door.

'Perhaps there's another source,' I said.

'Nothing's impossible,' agreed Magnon. 'Let's go to see what Bahni's on about.'

Bahni had been right. Where he stood the atmosphere was at its foulest. Instinctively Magnon and I recoiled. Bahni came over to us. 'I'm less used to good atmosphere than you two,' he said. 'Even so . . .'

We all looked at the spot where he had been standing.

'Maybe there's something in the cell,' I said.

122

'Let's look,' said Magnon.

Slowly, we went towards the source of the smell. It was worse than nauseous: it was frightening. My spine felt cold, and the hairs stood up on the back of my neck. I had felt less fear than this when facing capture or discovery, or even when observing the dreamstate sky crack open. This time, there was something within me telling me to fear. It was a voice I had not heard before, a voice at whose existence I had not even guessed. But now, as it told me to be frightened, I knew that it had always been a part of my being.

We stood at the door and looked at one another. I could see that the others felt the same. I had never expected to see bewilderment and terror manifest themselves so clearly in Magnon's eyes, but there they were, in abundance.

'We'll have to open the door,' I wheezed. 'Sooner the better.'

Magnon nodded, and leant forward to turn the handle.

The door swung inwards of its own volition. The stench billowed out. I could hear Bahni retching. So much, I thought, for his claim that he was more used to a foul atmosphere than I and Magnon.

Inhaling only when our bodies insisted, we made our way into the gloom.

The man sat awkwardly on his chair. Both his arms hung limply over the sides, and his legs were splayed oddly.

Mouth agape and eyes dull, he stared at the ceiling, his head thrown back. I had never seen anyone so still.

Cautiously I went over to him and touched his shoulder. As I withdrew my hand I touched his face. It did not feel as though it were of flesh.

Magnon came up and did the same, only more roughly. The man's body slipped a little and the head moved through a semi-circle before coming to rest with its chin on the man's chest.

Slowly at first, then with gathering momentum, the man bent forward on the chair and then rolled out of it before striking the floor with his head, which was still tucked well into his chest.

He half lay, half knelt for an instant. Then one of the legs straightened itself, pushing the rump higher and higher until the pyramid of body toppled over and hit the floor again.

His eyes were staring as fixedly out of the door as they had at the ceiling.

I had quite forgotten the stench. 'What is he?' I asked.

'He's dead,' said Magnon.

Death.

We knew that it would come, but we had not calculated on its effects. We were all, even Magnon, so accustomed to regarding it as a phenomenon that was kept out of sight, that we had been incapable of foreseeing its effects upon the living.

In normal times when a death occurred the event was dealt with quickly and with the minimum of fuss. It was one of the rules that a cadaver should be sent for reprocessing as soon after the departure of life as possible, in the way that garbage was disposed of the instant it became garbage.

And somehow this was always achieved.

But now the habitat was out of kilter. Even if the central administration computer had been informed of the man's death – which was improbable because his occupation of the cell was unlikely to have been registered – the guardians of the cells were unwilling or unable to perform their duties.

So the man died, and started to smell.

Without uttering we moved as a team towards the body, lifted it and carried it towards the garbage disposal unit. With a hiss and a click the door to the unit opened and we put him in.

For a few moments his legs waved above the level of the unit's rim and then slowly they sank. Magnon pushed the lid to. It failed to shut. He lifted it again, gave a shove to the foot that had got caught and slammed the lid again.

This time it closed properly, and the smell of death receded.

'Well, so much for that,' said Bahni.

Magnon and I looked at each other and grimaced.

I visualised the garbage belt littered with corpses, and remembered how little room there had been for my live body upon it. Should, say, a pair of bodies become entangled with each other down there the tunnel would become blocked.

'And then what would happen?' I asked aloud.

Bahni looked at me blankly, but Magnon seemed to understand.

'You mean if the garbage system became overloaded with corpses?' he said.

'Yes. Or just blocked?'

'Life would become very unpleasant. We knew what we were doing would make life unpleasant. We just didn't know what form the unpleasantness would take. Now it's working out.'

'Unpleasant, yes. But suppose it becomes impossible?'

'Well, again, we knew it would become impossible for some. Like that fellow down there.' He jerked his head towards the disposal unit. 'That was the idea, wasn't it? That was the meaning of all your words . . . a period of transition, leading to a new way of life?'

'Yes – but don't you see . . . life may become impossible for *all* of the living. And the transition could become a permanency. What then?'

I knew I was making sense to Magnon. Even Bahni looked scared.

'You're not regretting it?' asked Bahni. 'I mean . . . there's nothing you can do about it now.'

I shook my head. I don't know if I convinced Bahni. I didn't convince myself. And I don't think I convinced Magnon, although he said nothing.

Towards evening he left us. It was strange not having him with us any more.

II

DURING the next few days we did what we could to hasten the time when the new social order would emerge. Or that's what we told ourselves we were doing. In reality we were doing what we could to fend off disaster. Which was very little.

Many more died. Others grew weak and ill, either from a lack of oxygen or nutriment or both. Fortunately the supply of water, by some quirk of the system, kept up.

Most of the released Sleepees were very unhappy; as unhappy as the bewildered Texecs. The odour which follows death was to disgust and terrify the entire population, and added immeasurably to its burden.

'What makes that smell?' I asked. Gnofina answered. 'I think it's a process called decomposition,' she said. 'It's a process similar to the one used in the reprocessor units, except that it's natural, and uncontrolled.'

We shuddered. It sounded nasty.

Gnofina sounded almost apologetic, as she always did when she was obliged to reveal knowledge that was not common property to the company.

'I think it's caused by tiny living things. Very simple, and very small,' she said. 'Someone told me about it once. I think it was when I was in trouble for not putting surplus nutriment into the disposer straight away.'

Bahni and I looked at her and nodded. Instant disposal of organic waste was a rule that even the Sleepees were expected to adhere to strictly. It was seldom that someone failed to do this, but when they did, they were in trouble.

'I was quite young at the time and so the man didn't have me punished. He explained that these tiny things were the

126

reason why we had to throw everything away. "They shouldn't be allowed to grow" he said.'

'Well, if they're the cause of this death smell, he was quite right,' I said.

'Yes, but there was more to it than that. I think he said that these little things could sort of eat up live people too in certain circumstances. But then . . . I think he told me not to worry because the atmosphere conditioners dealt with them. So that's all right, isn't it?'

I didn't know, so I didn't say anything. Nor did Bahni. I could see that he was as worried as I was.

Neither of us had realized that there was anything other than humanity that could be described as living.

But after that it seemed to us that the rules relating to cleanliness in Cubale were somehow more significant than they ever had been, and we tried to pass this on to others.

From this point of view it was fortunate that organic waste was rare. Anything left lying around got eaten. As the days wore on the nutrition dispensers grew more niggardly; more people would die and would be sent down the garbage disposers. Some quickly, others less quickly.

Soon we could tell the sort of person that was most likely to die: he or she would be older than most, or perhaps be possessed of some deformity, or a feebleness, or a malfunction of some organ. Such disadvantages would be counted as no more than inconvenient in the times before the revolution, when demand was regulated to meet supply.

But now the forces of supply and demand were balancing themselves out, by eliminating the weakest in the demand force.

'I suppose,' said Bahni one morning, 'that enough people will be dying to supply the reprocessors with enough waste to feed the living.'

I was getting ready to go out into the corridors to talk, once more, to the people, to see if there were any chance yet of organising them.

'You're right,' I said. 'The point is – are they going to wait long enough for that to happen? They don't know enough about death . . . everyone thinks that it will be his turn to die next. We must try and tell them what is happening. Come on.'

'I don't think you should. Not any more.' Gnofina, so brave herself, so cowardly on my behalf. She stood up and her short, plump person assumed its own kind of dignity.

'But we must,' I said. 'You know we must.'

Bahni, who had risen to leave, sat down again.

'There's no point. They don't listen to you.'

'But they will – at least they *may* – one day. And then, this place Cubale will start living once more.'

'They may. They may not. But once they learn that you are to blame for their plight, you'll be in trouble. You'll be in great danger.'

'I won't be if they understand why we've done what we did. And they'll never understand that if I don't go out and tell them.'

'But it's dangerous!'

'It may be if I don't go out to them.'

'It's dangerous *now*. I've got a feeling.'

'How can it possibly be? They are all still numb with it all. Even the former Texecs. They're not capable . . .'

'And Magnon? Is he not capable?'

Suddenly I saw what she meant. She had never taken to Magnon. I had hated him, then loved him. But there had never been anything like that between her and him. Just a mutual indifference and mistrust.

They had worked well together though because, I think, of me. So they had come to know each other well too. But with knowledge had come an increasing wariness between the two. They had never spoken about it. But I knew.

'You never liked Magnon,' I said.

'You must admit he left very suddenly. There was no explanation. We haven't seen a trace of him since. Or of his friends. That is strange,' she said.

I shrugged. 'Yes, I admit it. Now I'm going out. Come on, Bahni.'

I went to the door, turned the handle, and pulled.

No matter how hard I tried, it would not open. When I rattled it, I could hear it shaking against the steel bar that had been fixed to it on the outside.

'We're locked in,' I said. 'We're locked in.' It was a stupid thing to say, but I couldn't help saying it.

I looked at Gnofina. 'We . . .' I began.

'We're locked in,' she said. 'Why not try your credit key?' she added sarcastically.

I went back to the door and hammered on it, and shouted. 'You won't do any good like that,' she said. 'If they're going to lock us in, they aren't going to let us out just because you're making a silly noise, are they?'

'No.'

I stared out of the peephole in the door. It gave a widish vision, but I could see no one.

'Who's done this?' I said.

'Magnon. Remember?'

'Ah, don't be ridiculous. Why should he do a thing like that?'

'I expect he'll tell you,' said Gnofina. 'He's vain enough to want to. I don't suppose it's any use telling you that you don't have to listen to him?'

'No,' I said. 'Not that this has anything to do with him. I shall simply wait.'

She laughed, sat down at the table, and began to write. Bahni, who was sitting on the bed, took out a pack of cards from an inside pocket and flourished them at me in invitation.

Wearily, I shrugged consent and sat down next to him. He loved his cards.

The hours passed. Once or twice we actually got the nutriment dispenser to work. After a while, even Bahni grew tired of cards and dozed. Gnofina continued to write. Then I dozed, too.

Once or twice I awoke when I thought I heard something, but most of the time I slept. I suppose I was becoming immune to the prospect of disaster.

A banging on the door awoke me. I lay there for an

instant. Nothing pleasant would result from my arising, and I could see no purpose in getting up in a hurry.

The banging continued.

'Come on, come on!' he shouted.

I smiled to myself. So Gnofina had been right after all. I suppose I had refused to admit even to myself that Magnon had been responsible for locking us in. For with him against us, we had little to hope for.

Nevertheless I smiled. By refusing to leap up at his peremptory summons I had made him lose face by shouting at me.

My expression must have been pleasant as I unfolded myself from the bed and sat up to look at the eyes in the grille, for they looked astonished. Then angry.

'What are you grinning at?' he said.

'You, of course.'

Plainly he expected me to register fear, fury, bewilderment, indignation . . . anything but amusement.

I continued to smile.

'Come here.'

'Certainly. But why don't you come in? You have the key, surely?'

'Of course I do. I don't want to come in.'

He sounded petulant. I assumed that he was playing a role for an audience other than myself. My attitude was unhelpful.

I continued to be unhelpful.

'In that case, my dear Magnon, I shall come to *you*.'

I walked over towards the door. Just before I finished walking, just as he was drawing breath to speak, I spoke.

'Yes?'

Instead of speaking, he merely exhaled. Even his way of breathing registered annoyance. He drew breath again in praparation for speech, and this time he succeeded.

'It has been decided that in the interests of the general good you should be forbidden access to public places until further notice,' he said.

'Right,' I said. 'Is that all?'

I was determined not to stay at the grille for long, so while I was there I made the best of it. I looked from side to side of Magnon's head, which blocked most of the view through the small aperture. But I had been able to see that there were indeed several people with him – including some of the youngsters whom he had brought into our team in the early days of the revolution.

'Yes, that's all,' he said. As he spoke the words I turned my back on him and, feigning indifference, made my way back to the bed.

With a grunt he withdrew from the grille, slammed it shut, and barked some unintelligible orders. The response to these orders was strange: it sounded as though feet were being stamped in unison, and then being made to walk all at once, the several footfalls coming precisely together, to a measured step, in a regulated time.

I was tempted to get up to the grille to see what Magnon's men were doing, but resisted. My diffidence had put him at a disadvantage when all the initiative should have been his.

It was not, as Gnofina had indicated, to satisfy his vanity that Magnon had come to crow over me: it was to establish a position, prove a point, demonstrate that he was the master.

My lack of desire for an explanation was not entirely assumed.

It was clear that the things I had been saying to people were dangerous: notions of a society run by all its members, to which everyone contributed, in which a life was lived more according to personal inclination than to official decree, and other crazy ideas were almost by definition dangerous where there was an establishment.

And although there was now no establishment in Cubale, Magnon was obviously trying to create one.

I had hoped that a society would emerge from the revolutionary chaos that would be on the lines of my preaching. But this was obviously impossible; I did not blame Magnon.

And I knew exactly what he wanted now. So I needed no explanation.

The machines which supplied the material needs of our habitat in Cubale had failed to recover rapidly enough from the strains thrown upon them by the social changes. As I was to learn later, it was inevitable that they should fail to do so; but in the meantime the population was in great distress: undernourished, overcrowded, insecure, closer to death than ever before. Many Sleepees had lost their reason through stumber withdrawal, and the cries of the mad ones aggravated the already acute discomfort of the sane.

The fears that Magnon and I had felt about the garbage tunnels seizing up had become widespread, and those who were already short of nutrition found it easy to imagine the horrors of a water shortage.

Far from being an ideal society in the making, in Cubale there was a human menagerie on the brink of self-destruction.

No, I could not blame Magnon for his impatience. In his eyes, he was justified in deserting me to set up his own organisation. Really, I had no organisation. Merely a genius for disorganisation. At least I had achieved my main object: to free the Sleepees. There could be no going back to the caverns now in Cubale.

Or so I thought.

And again, I slept. I learned later that when this simple action was reported to Magnon, he was thrown into such a state of confusion and fury that he was unable to think about me calmly for several days afterwards.

But there were plenty of other decisions for him to take. He was welcome to them.

After my time-buying slumber, still unaware that I was being observed, I arose and searched the system of inter-communicating cells that we had established.

I was quite alone.

But I could no more blame Gnofina for deserting me than I could blame Magnon.

Provided always, of course, that she had deserted me . . .

I could hear steps outside, going nowhere. Just walking up and down the corridor outside. Guarding me.

The door opened for the first time in a week and closed again with a bang. I did not have to look round to know that it was Gnofina.

I felt her hand upon my shoulder. Then it slid towards my neck, up, paused on the top of my head, where it made a vague circular motion before descending to my forehead, where again it moved, but from side to side.

'Poor Phillips,' she said.

'Alas,' I said.

'They let me come and see you,' she said.

'They?' I said.

'Well, Magnon, really,' she said.

'How kind,' I said.

'Yes,' she said. 'It was, wasn't it?'

There was something in her voice which made me look up, but there was nothing decipherable in her expression, so I looked away again.

'And, I know he wants to see you himself, but he's so busy.'

Again I looked up, but still there was nothing to see. I decided to listen to the inflexions of Gnofina's voice very carefully.

'Already you can see the difference now he's taken over. He's got these young men, you see, telling people what to do, how to organize themselves to make life better. And he's getting all the maintenance people to report for duty at headquarters, too. And if they don't come, boy, are they in trouble.'

This wasn't Gnofina talking. It was her voice, but they weren't her words.

I tried a question.

'And the Sleepee cavern controllers. I suppose he's got them back at work, too?'

She looked at me quickly, as though in warning. But warning me of what?

'Well, really, the poor people have to sleep somewhere,' she said. 'I mean, half of them are back in the caverns already. It's simply a question of comfort.'

'Stumber makes you comfortable,' I said.

Again she looked at me. This time it was as though she was pleading with me. *Shut your mouth you fool,* she seemed to be saying, *for my sake, if not for your own.*

'Oh, nothing like that,' she said aloud, too brightly. 'It's just like I said – they have to have somewhere to sleep and, really, the caverns have to be used.'

'By Texecs too?'

'I don't know.'

'I bet you don't.'

Then she kissed me.

'Oh, Phillips,' she said, as though it had been I who kissed her.

I felt resentful, and was disinclined at first to make love. But she knew me better than I knew myself and within minutes I was fumbling with her body, starting a voyage of exploration in which route and destination would yield a fresh thrill of discovery each time.

In the shower afterwards she poked me in the navel with a finger. It hurt. 'It was meant to,' she hissed above the noise of the water. 'They were listening to everything we said. And they were watching too.' And she smiled sweetly. 'That's in case they can see in here, too,' she said. 'At least they can't hear.'

She went on: 'Magnon's setting himself up as a ruler. That's fine by me, but I know you won't like it. He's also going to allow any Sleepee who wants to revert to his old status to do so.'

My bellow of indignation was blocked once more with an expert kiss.

'Easy,' she said. 'Again, I don't mind. But I know you won't like it. Anyway he let me come hoping that I could talk you into joining him. He says he would have more moral force with you on his side. But if you're against him, he'll have to get rid of you somehow. He's scared of you.'

I shrugged. The steam rose about us. At least water was still plentiful. And the power was returning.

'Perhaps you don't care, but I do. I'm sure he wouldn't hesitate to put you into the garbage reprocessor if you were in his way. So you either join him or you risk death.'

'Death,' I said, smiling, not believing her.

'Or you leave Cubale, and maybe come back later to fight again.'

She pretended to concentrate on washing her thighs as she went on. 'There's a way out behind the shower room two cells down. I made it myself when I saw this situation coming weeks ago.'

'You must come with me,' I said.

She looked at me and smiled. 'I've got to,' she said. 'Only I know the way. But I'm glad you wanted me to come anyhow.'

I couldn't quite figure out why, but somehow I felt as though I *needed* her, that I would rather stay here and face whatever was coming to me than leave Cubale without her. It was nothing to do with her common sense, her resourcefulness, her knowledge of the way the Texecs lived that made me feel I needed her, although all that had helped, time and time again. It was something else.

Perhaps, I thought, if I could understand myself, I would be able to understand the problems facing the revolutionary habitat of Cubale.

After the shower, Gnofina left. We agreed that the timing of the escape should be left to her. It was clear that we should have to delay it by a few days, for Magnon, who had sent her to me as an emissary, would – quite rightly – have doubts about her loyalty to him and would be watching her closely.

But we felt that it would not be too long before something distracted him – and that would be the time to make a dash for it.

In the meantime we would have to hope that he would leave me alone in the cell to ponder his offer. Doubtless he would welcome any excuse to delay his decision over me.

135

After a few days it seemed that our hope was to be fulfilled. I spoke to no one, saw no one. I had nothing to do but sit by the nutriment dispenser and try to coax it into yielding a bit more.

At first I was relieved, and then perplexed, and then worried as more days wore on with no sign from Gnofina. Should I continue to risk waiting for her? Or should I make the break on my own?

Apart from any emotional disinclination to the latter course, it was obvious that I should stand a much better chance having Gnofina with me.

My imagination flourished in the loneliness of the cell. All kinds of horrors presented themselves to me as possibilities. Melancholy prevailed; far from feeling perpetually hungry, I found that the nutriment was nauseating, and had to force myself to eat.

One night, shortly after the illumination had been dimmed, I lay on the bed sleeping uneasily. Suddenly in my unconsciousness I felt that someone was standing over me, watching me.

He grew huge and menacing. His arms extended themselves and writhed around my prone and helpless form. The creature's head seemed to inflate, leaving the eyes central and small. They bored into my being, and hooked themselves immoveably on to my mind.

It spoke without the agency of a mouth. The words boomed and echoed in the vast and empty chambers of its cranium, which now enveloped me.

'Jim, Jim, silly little Sleepee,' it said. 'Did you think you could turn the world upside down?' Its breathing was enormous. With each passing second great quantities of air were sucked down into its rapacious lungs, whistling and howling along its gullet and, befouled, was expelled to make way for more.

'Did you think that you could alter the preordained nature of things? Would you make the Sleepees Texecs and the Texecs Sleepees? And have you learned it cannot be

136

done? Have you changed Cubale just for the worse, creating misery where there was once pleasure, installing a despot where there was once rule by committee and computer? Did you? Did? Did?'

I tried to reply but found that the words would not come. I knew that I was dreaming, but it was a dream that could continue into reality if I failed to escape from it. I cast my mind back to the dreamstate of my Lemington days, but it was disastrous. I was able to recollect only the cracking sky. And then I found that the roof of the imprisoning cranium had turned into the sky and that the crack was wide enough to permit the entry of the scream . . . .

'Easy, easy, easy.' It was a cool and soothing voice in the darkness. A cloth of some sort was being used to wipe the sweat from my face; a firm hand bore down upon my flailing forearm. I sobbed, opened my mouth to scream again, and awoke.

'Bahni!' I said. 'It's you. I . . . I was . . .'

'I know,' he said. 'I can recognize a bad dream when I see one.' Sleepees knew about bad dreams and dreaded them. It was a bad dream long ago that had got me where I was now. They were right to dread bad dreams.

'How are you?' Bahni's voice was sympathetic.

I told him.

'I'm sorry,' he said. 'I meant to come and see you before, but it's risky, you understand, very risky, and besides . . .' He stopped. Even in the dark I could tell he was excited.

'Well?' I said. 'Besides what?'

'Well, it's this sex thing that everybody's found out about. I wanted to do as much as I could before they took it away again. I've been selfish, I'm sorry, but I couldn't resist it.'

'Of course not.' By now I had recovered my wits. But – it was obvious! Why should I be alone in recovering my sex as a result of a stumber withdrawal? It was inevitable that nearly all Sleepees would do the same.

By now, Cubale would be one heaving mass of enthusiastic copulation.

I laughed, sat up and slapped Bahni on the shoulder. 'Of course I understand,' I said again. 'It's very good of you to come at all. But you need the rest, eh? So you came to see me instead?'

He nodded, quite seriously. 'Yes, I think I do need a rest. But I think I'll be getting all I need soon.'

'Why's that? Anyway, why should they take it away again?'

'Well, they say Magnon doesn't approve. He says he's going to have to put everybody back on stumber.'

'Why?'

Bahni said: 'Well, this sex thing . . . it's supposed to make new people, you see. Magnon reckons that in less than a year, there are going to be nearly a third as many people again as there are now in Cubale.'

I groaned. The consequences of sex, like the consequences of death, had simply never entered into my thinking. I had been kept ignorant of them, like any other Sleepee, for most of my life; even in Lemington when I came out of the dormys the Texecs tried to perpetuate my ignorance about them while they expanded my learning in other fields.

And I hadn't thought about it much in Cubale. I suppose that if I had applied myself I could have acquired enough knowledge to be forewarned, but somehow I had been too concerned with other things. Why had I not been forewarned?

Magnon. He *must* have known. Why then did he execute the revolution?

The misery that would result from the introduction into Cubale of all those new people would be intolerable. He must have known.

He must have.

Therefore, he must have planned it. He had used me simply to further his own position. He had had complete control over a large number of Sleepees, but this was not enough. He wanted all the Sleepees and also all his fellow

Texecs under him. And he had used me to realize his ambition. My disgrace was complete.

And my future?

Bahni answered my unspoken question. 'At least you're safe for the time being,' he said. 'At the moment you're a hero. You're the man who led the Sleepees to sex.'

'Is that how they think of me now?' I smiled. 'It's quite an enviable reputation. What happens to it when the new people come?'

'They can't blame you for that.'

'If they can praise me for the discovery of sex, then they can blame me for its results, Bahni. It's as logical as that.'

'Yes.' In the darkness I could see him nodding agreement. 'But they won't.'

'What of Gnofina?'

'Well, she's with Magnon a lot of the time. They seem very friendly. Perhaps she's making up to him so that she can protect you, I don't know.' Then he leaned forward and whispered quickly: 'They'll think that's a lie, but it isn't.' It was plain he knew we were being overheard.

'Perhaps she is,' I said. 'Then maybe Magnon's making up to *her* to threaten *me*.' Sometimes the less you said the better. Sometimes the more you said, the better.

Bahni was beginning to be restless. 'You'd better go,' I said. 'You don't want to waste any more time in here when you could be out there copulating.'

He pretended to protest, but I could tell that he was relieved.

'Well, Bahni, I guess the best thing I can do is to wait around here and see what happens. If I were to make a break for it, I'd have nowhere to go. At least this place is fairly comfortable . . .'

He broke in: 'Nowhere to go is right. Since some of the Texecs tried to leave Cubale, Magnon's made it so that only he and a few of his lieutenants can call tuberockets now. Entry permits were difficult enough – but exit is impossible.'

'Go on,' I said, pretending to be unimpressed. 'Remember me to Lieutenant Gnofina.'

He laughed. 'Sure,' he said.

He left after making a promise to return soon.

Later, I looked through the grille to the corridor outside. For the first time there were no guards out there. Maybe it was coincidence. Maybe it wasn't, but suddenly they appeared to be less concerned about me making an attempt at escape.

I slept easier after that and spent a quiet day writing and dozing and wiping my face with a damp red cloth in the hope that some of its dye would transfer itself to my skin.

When the illuminations dimmed to herald the night, I left the cell through Gnofina's secret door and felt free for the first time in weeks.

I was apprehensive when I first left the little service passageway at the back of the cells and turned into a main thoroughfare.

But after a short while my fears left me. Even if I had failed to darken my face effectively, few would have noticed me. Where previously the walkways had been littered with prone, apathetic bewildered Sleepees, it was now littered with couples, all totally absorbed in one another.

Most of them were quite open about their actions; a few here and there groped at each other furtively under a covering of rags, but for the most part there was none of that modesty which characterized the sexual behaviour of the Texec.

I found all this activity fascinating and was reminded that it was many days since I had had sex myself. Surely there would be no risk of . . . In fact if I wanted to be more inconspicuous than I already was I would *have* to find myself a girl.

There were some unattached people in the corridors, although not many. And of those most were Texecs, and not necessarily looking for sex partners.

But I was bound to find a single Sleepee female sooner or later. And if they were all as anxious about sex as Bahni

140

had indicated, any offer I chose to make was likely to be accepted.

But first find the single female. . . .

She was a plain creature, but not too old. She stood there in the middle of the corridor, feet apart, hands on hips, watching my approach. It was as though she had been waiting for me.

Perhaps she was on her own because others found her unattrative, I felt, and I asked her if she were free.

We walked along, hand in hand (an inconvenient but not unpleasant way of making progress) stepping over the bodies as we went along. An old man, watching the couples looked up as we passed by, but I could not see his face in the shadow.

Soon I got her to talk about herself – thus relieving me of the obligation to talk about myself – and I learned that far from being alone because of the meagreness of her form and the irregularity of her features, she was solitary through choice.

'I like to change partners once or twice a day,' she said. 'And you have a better chance of getting a new one if you're on your own. So after a short while I leave the man. I get another one pretty quickly as a rule. Most people like a change. I just like a change more than most people. Anyway – let's stop wandering around and get to know each other better.''

I didn't want to lose her, but at the same time, I didn't want to do it in front of all the others. Perhaps it was the Texec training holding me back.

'No,' I said. 'Not yet. It's better if you wait a little bit longer than you want to.'

'Is it?' She was interested by this idea, which was plainly new to her.

So we continued walking and talking until we got to the tubeport, by which time we were both breathless. Surreptitiously I operated Magnon's credit key, and the door slid open. We stepped through. The port was quite empty. I pulled the door to behind me.

'Now?' she said.

'Now,' I said. But we had to get our breath back first.

Then the girl and I had coupled with the urgency of people who know that time is running out on them. After a strenuous hour or two we drew apart, although not very far apart, and rested.

We lay on a bench that had its back to the entrance so that the woman who came in and went straight over to the tuberocket schedule board did not see us.

I listened to her voice as she made inquiries, and the buzzing sound of the relayed replies. Gradually it occurred to me that her voice was familiar.

'Gnofina!' I said, and sat up.

She looked round, startled, and came towards me.

Then she went back to the board and punched some controls.

'You're crazy,' she said.

'True,' I said, feeling foolishly smug.

'You've ruined everything,' she went on. 'Now you'll have to leave straight away, and I can't go yet.'

Her eyes filled with tears. 'You'll just have to get on this tuberocket and chance your being able to get off. You can't stay here now. Magnon's made up his mind . . .' She stopped.

The girl had sat up, too.

Gnofina's face changed colour. First red, then white. She took a few short, ungainly, rapid steps forward with her arms above her head, her fingers crooked like talons and her nails pointing at me, and at the girl.

Then she stopped, grunted, paused as though for thought, turned on her heels and made for the door. She went outside and slammed it behind her.

After what felt like a long time, the girl and I began to breathe again. 'What got into her?' she said. 'I just can't imagine,' I said, and I couldn't.

Quickly I scrambled into my clothes again. 'I think I'd better go after her,' I told the girl. 'Thanks, anyway.'

142

'See you again, maybe,' she said. 'You seem to know what you're doing.'

There was an invitation in her casual praise, but I didn't listen. I was more worried about Gnofina. Perhaps she was ill. I had to go after her.

I went to the door and pulled. The locking lever would not budge. Either it had failed or . . . Gnofina had locked us in. But why?

Still in a daze, but remembering her apparent fury, I fastened *my* side of the door by up-ending one of the benches and leaning it against the lever, so that it would take a great effort from the other side to shift it.

'What are you doing *now*?' asked the girl. I had almost forgotten she was there. 'I don't quite know. Buying time perhaps. Something nasty's going to happen, and I want to put it off as long as possible,' I said.

Oddly enough, she seemed satisfied.

'Once more, then,' she said. Wearily, locked in again after such a little freedom, I lay down beside her.

But soon, above the sound of her breathing was the rattle of the door lever being twisted to and fro by someone who was determined to get in.

Then everything seemed to happen at once. There was that roaring shrieking sound made by an approaching tube-rocket, and a cry of triumph from the men on the other side of the door, which began to slide open.

Through the gap I could see three or four men – two of them I recognized as Magnon's henchmen – and Gnofina.

As they stepped through the gap, I rolled off the startled girl onto the trembling floor. I picked myself up just as the sudden comparative quiet indicated that the tuberocket had arrived. I ran straight towards the convex wall with Gnofina's men in pursuit and as I came up to it, the door in it began to run back on its guides.

As soon as the gap was wide enough, I slipped through, and once on the other side, pushed against it as hard as I could.

I was taking a chance. I knew that the door was geared so

that it could not be opened from the outside under normal operating conditions. The checks and balances of the mechanism were arranged against the inadvertent *opening* of the door, for if the door were open at the wrong time, then the entire atmosphere of a habitat could be sucked into the vacuum tube – with disastrous effects on both tube and habitat.

But the risks attached to the door being *shut* at the wrong time were relatively small.

So I pushed, and hoped for the best.

And, sure enough, the door began to slide forward again. Then it stopped. The men on the other side had reached it, and were pushing against me. I heaved, and they heaved.

One against four, and I held my ground. I had been right – the balancing mechanism of the door *was* to my advantage. The designers had done their job well.

All five of us were panting with the exertion. My head felt as though it was about to burst. My hold upon consciousness was beginning to slacken but Gnofina's voice, urging the men to greater efforts, helped me to think clearly once again.

It was plain that this could not go on for ever. Eventually I would be beaten: either the overriding controls in the tubeport would be operated and the door would be opened that way, or simply, they would get more men to keep the door open and would wait until I had to give in.

Either way, it was a matter of time. I looked quickly towards the tuberocket. The entrance was invitingly open.

I let go the door and dashed for the rocket.

Once inside, I ignored the attendant and hunted rapidly among the controls by the entrance. There was a stud marked 'Close' and I pressed it. Nothing happened. Doubtless the automatic 'Close' was inhibited by the fact that the main door from the tubeport was opened.

But there was nothing to prevent me from shutting the tuberocket door manually, was there? I grabbed the handle and heaved.

'Oi!' said the attendant. I pushed with all my flagging strength. Inch by inch the door slid forward.

I could see the first of Gnofina's men start to squeeze himself through the main door, now slowly opening. My door gathered momentum. It accelerated towards the seal which would make opening it from the outside an impossibility.

There was a sudden slight roughness in its motion towards the seal as though it had engaged a switch. And sure enough, the door into the tubeport started once more to close. The man's mouth went agape and his eyes started as it began to grip him.

As I strained against my door, so the gap opposite continued to narrow. The rocket hatch was a master for the tuberocket door. My efforts were being reproduced and magnified by the mechanism designed to ensure that the vacuum of the tube and the atmosphere of the habitat would never meet.

The man started to scream but suddenly the noise stopped and he was quiet. He went very thin and then a great bubble seemed to sprout the length of his flank.

Just as I was about to shut the hatch completely something slapped it on the outside. Then I heard the seal click to and I felt a warmth about my lower legs.

I let go of the lever and looked down.

From my knees to my feet I was saturated with blood. Just on the side facing the door.

Silently, the attendant strapped me in, bloody legs and all, just as though all his passengers came in covered in gore. Maybe he thought he'd better humour me. Perhaps he thought that if I could kill once, I could kill twice.

But if he was deliberately playing the matter down, he was playing it down very effectively.

I tried to be kind and warm. I needed him to be a friend. 'I'm glad you came when you did. It was a pleasant surprise,' I said.

'You mean it wasn't you who called us specially?' he asked. 'We don't stop at Cubale these days unless we're called in specially, you know. I thought it must have been you, seeing that you were in such a hurry.'

He too was trying to be friendly with me. Just then it didn't really matter why. He was telling me a lot. He was telling me more than I knew, but I didn't find that out until later.

'When did you get the call?'

'About twenty minutes ago.'

'Well, we'd better go, before it's cancelled.'

I didn't want Gnofina's men outside to find a way in again. I wanted to get away. But would Gnofina really stop me, considering she'd called in the rocket specially for me? I wondered.

Smiling to myself, I braced against the lateral G which accompanied our departure.

When the G eased, I unstrapped myself and went over to the attendant.

'Sorry you had such a fright back there,' I smiled. 'They were after me, you see. I didn't know that fellow would get trapped like that. I didn't know that would happen.'

He nodded. 'Well, there's funny things you hear about Cubale these days,' he said. 'I suppose almost anything can happen. I know just one thing.' He looked at me keenly. 'I never want to go there. In fact, I never want to go anywhere but Burmagem. Burmagem's my home habitat.'

So much for my new society, I thought bitterly.

'Here,' said the attendant. 'Would you like to wash those legs?'

'Thanks.' He showed me the shower cubicle.

'Help yourself. But don't be too long. We haven't a long time before Blasintium.'

Blasintium? I had heard vaguely of the place. I recalled vaguely the Lemington Texecs speaking of it in terms of a sort of scandalised admiration. I had felt that they envied their fellows there, but disapproved of them at the same time.

But maybe my memories were wrong. It all seemed so long ago . . .

'Come on now,' said the attendant, not unkindly, as I washed the last of the blood from me. 'Blasintium in five minutes.'

Blasintium?

Why Blasintium?

Was it just that the attendant wanted his blood-soaked passenger off his rocket at the first stop, or . . .

'Why Blasintium?' I said.

'Well, that's where you're going, isn't it?'

'Is it?'

'That's what it says here.' He nodded towards the journeyscreen. I glanced at it, noticed the phrase: 'Payment, credit against . . .' when it went blank, and gave out a high-pitched warbling.

'That's it,' he said. 'Back on the pad.'

Why had Gnofina sent me to Blasintium, I wondered. And was it she who was paying for the trip? The name on the board didn't look like hers.

And why Blasintium?

'Pretty place Blasintium, so they say,' said the attendant.

But she wouldn't have had time to programme the destination, not back there in the tubeport.

Maybe this was another put-up job to deceive me.

But why?

12

IT was, as the attendant had said, a pretty place. Nobody stopped me as I walked straight from the tubeport into a great open area. I felt welcome in the light and spaciousness of it and breathed the sweet atmosphere with relish. The air was more than oxygen-rich; it bestowed upon me an olfactory pleasure.

147

The experience was unique. I shall always remember my entry into Blasintium with pleasure, even though now when I encounter the smell that was put into that air, I want to vomit.

The sky over this open place was cunningly fashioned and perfectly maintained so that to the casual eye it appeared infinite. It gave off no reflection, nor did it bear a shadow.

In this sky there was a single light source, extremely bright, that somehow caused the shadows to be thrown in the same proportions, direction and intensity throughout the area.

The immediate effect of this extraordinary phenomenon was to give rise to a sense of well-being, almost of euphoria.

In the square there was a number of people in small groups, sauntering about or at rest. They were, I felt, extremely attractive, the women being clothed in garments reaching from shoulder to ankle, tight about the torso but loose from the waist down, in pale and charming colours and of a texture giving somehow a flowing account of their movements.

The men, mostly tall and dark, wore clothes of more vivid hues. Scarlets and deep blues and purples were popular among them. They wore tunics, and breeches which ended at the knee. Their lower legs were encased in tight-fitting white garments and white, too, was the colour of the adornment about their throats.

These men wore their hair long, pulled back neatly from the face and fastened at the nape of the neck. The women's hairstyles were amazingly generous, with great curls and ringlets descending in ordered profusion over their bosoms and their shoulders. As they talked and moved their proliferating ringlets echoed their gestures most gracefully. I was entranced by all the elegance.

My wet legs, my shabby and meagre one-piece, my ungainly demeanour at first made me feel awkward and ashamed.

But after a few moments my sense of discomfiture

vanished, for although none of these people actually greeted me I felt strangely welcome and as though I belonged to their queer and beautiful habitat.

In the centre of the square about eighty paces from where I stood was a device in white stone, a small, elegant artifact of intriguing shape, measuring about six feet across its flat base. Rising from the centre of the base was an oblong, with circular discs attached to four of its corners on one of its two wider sides, and a large central bump arising centrally opposite. What was most remarkable about this arrangement was the jet of water rising into the air from the top of the oblong and falling into the base which I could now see was a sort of bath.

I walked towards this marvellous object scarcely noticing the discomfort of my damp legs and as I drew nearer, I could see that to one side of it stood a cluster of objects which in their own way were just as remarkable. From the tubeport exit I had thought of them as large cushions, but now I was nearer I could see that they were much too frail to sustain any weight.

Their outer covering was composed of hundreds of tiny green slivers, so close together that they presented the eye at a distance with a uniform surface. These slivers were attached to minute sticks which were in turn themselves attached to larger sticks, several of each, and so on, until the sticks were joined ultimately to a central stick which itself was rooted in the ground.

Lost to all else, I stood before these things and marvelled. Slowly, without removing my eyes from them, I sunk to the ground and sat cross legged and regarded them, scarcely breathing.

There was more to them than their singularity. Somehow these things were deeply significant. But of what? There was a particularly powerful symbolism in the little jet of water that fell from the pipe at the top of the sculpture to splash the complex that stood in the ground next to it.

There was meaning there, but I could not read it. I had seen it all before, but where? Perhaps, I thought, it was something to do with the giving of life, for the green thing appeared somehow to be living. Just why I felt this I did not know: its form somehow was alien; too complex yet too simple, it resembled something that had been built from within rather than from without, rather in the way that my own body had been.

But certainly I felt no kinship with the object. Indeed the statue bubbling out water from its top addressed me more directly.

And yet I knew that it held a legitimate place within my consciousness. Somehow it reminded me of the ladders on the island I used to dream about back in Lemington. It was not that they resembled it but somehow I felt that they should have resembled it.

How long I sat there I do not know. I was oblivious to everything but these objects until I was disturbed by the sense of heat upon the top of my head. I looked up and saw that the light source had been shifted and was now directly above.

I had not realized before that it was a source of heat as well, but now I knew. I covered the top of my head with my hands to protect it and as I did so, became aware of a pair of feet before me.

Elegantly shod, they gave way to a pair of white shiny shins which in turn supported a set of purple-clad tights. Up and up I looked, only to find that the light source dazzled me and prevented me from seeing the man's face.

So I stood up, a little stiff, and looked at him, saying nothing.

'Take this,' he said. 'It gets hot at this time of day.' He held out a large floppy white hat, which I took and, mumbling my thanks, put it on my head.

The relief was instant. A bath of coolness enveloped my skull, my face and my shoulders. I looked at the man again and saw that he himself wore no hat.

Seeing my glance, he smiled. 'I'm used to it,' he said. 'Strangers always find our simsun a trifle irksome at first, though.'

'Of course,' I said, assuming that the light source above us was the simsun he spoke about. 'Thank you.'

'Not,' he continued, 'that we have many strangers these days. A few regular visitors, naturally, but very few people who come here for the first time. Rules and regulations make travel so difficult, do they not? I suppose you are a special case?'

'Yes,' I said. I wondered if he would ever know how special. Indeed, from what he said, I guessed that I was lucky to be here at all. By what fluke did I slip through the regulations restricting travel? Perhaps I would never know myself.

My head was beginning to swim. I realized that I was very weak. The lack of nutriment, the danger, the bewilderment of Blasintium were all too much for me.

The man's face, kindly, concerned, swung round in front of me, above me, behind me, loomed huge, then tiny, then blackness.

'Drink this.' The liquid was warm and sweet. I spluttered, sat up, fell back again. 'Where?' I said.

'In my home,' he said. 'My wife and I will look after you. You have been neglecting yourself.'

Even then, I found his remark amusing. I smiled at the man. Behind him there was a blurred figure in pink, who was, I assumed, the wife he spoke of.

Uncaring, I slumbered.

What the Edomands, for that was the name the couple shared, thought of me, I never discovered.

They seemed simply to accept me without question. And I was happy not to question their acceptance.

The less they learned about me, the happier they were. Sometimes when I spoke to them about myself, and what I had done in Lemington and Cubale, they seemed to switch off, to feign deafness, to deliberately misunderstand my words.

The Edomands were both immensely kind, yet somehow contrived to convey the impression that I did not really

151

exist as a viable individual. To them I was, I felt, simply an adjunct to their household.

Their attitude to Sleepees was also strange. Whenever I mentioned the word 'Sleepee' their expressions became blank, as though I had been indiscreet, and though they pretended not to know what the word Sleepee meant, invariably they changed the subject if I ever raised it.

Eventually I learned to live with their attitudes, and knew that domestic harmony could be achieved only by my avoiding mention of my history and my type.

I gave up trying to probe the reasons for their attitude and contented myself with the observation of Blasintium.

The most remarkable aspect of the place was the total absence of the Sleepees. For reasons I have already explained, I was unable to discover by questioning where, or indeed if, they lived in this particular habitat.

The Texecs of Blasintium lived well. Their existence was gentle and uncompetitive. Their habitat seemed sparsely populated and there was more than enough good atmosphere for everyone.

The place had ceased to develop. They had had their simulated sun for as long as anyone could remember, and they regarded it as the ultimate amenity: so long as it was maintained efficiently, they needed nothing more.

They were permitted limitless quantities of nutriment and water, and somehow the balance of reprocessing was weighted in favour of consumables. Often there was a surplus which had to go back to reprocessing without the intervention of consumption. How this was achieved was a mystery to me at the time, although it was to be horribly resolved later.

The inhabitants passed their time in study and in play. They had invented elaborate games of skill and would frequently spend days over just a small part of one competition. Also they pursued knowledge of what they called the 'old world' relentlessly: their knowledge seemed largely invented, but what was most interesting to me was that the concept could exist of a world preceding the present one.

But I kept my curiosity under control, as I always did with the Texecs, no matter how mannerly and gentle they might be. I did not find out much about the 'old world' with which they professed such concern, except that it yielded limitless space and an infinite quantity of breathable atmosphere, that there were many other forms of life upon it apart from mankind and that man had little or no control over his environment.

I heard of other fancies and there were many more which I did not hear about. But it was easy to see why the Blasintium Texecs found the idea so stimulating.

The old world offered everything that ours had not. The things that were most precious to us here were there in abundance without end. There was freedom to move about to excite the body and there were physical dangers to stimulate the spirit. There were – and this was immensely difficult to conceive – different elements to inhabit, and varied environments which were controlled by something outside humanity.

Whoever had first proposed the 'old world' idea was a genius; one could spend a lifetime speculating over it without approaching the end of its possibilities.

The days in Blasintium passed pleasantly enough for me, although from time to time I was uneasily aware that I was being observed, not by the Edomands, but by a shadowy thing that gave the impression of squatness and of unbelieveably smooth movements. It slid around the objects with which the Texecs in Blasintium liked to decorate their wide corridors and disappeared, and turned out of one corridor into another to vanish.

From time to time when I thought I had noticed it, I would ask my companions casually if they had noticed anything strange. But inevitably they would deny that they had.

There was an old man who was given to sitting in the public places of Blasintium, particularly on the seats in the main square, but sometimes in the corridors. On a number of occasions when I felt that this strange creature had been watching me I had seen the old man sitting nearby, staring vacantly into the distance. Once or twice I had thought of asking him, but in my position it was best to avoid approaching a Texec uninvited.

One of the games employed by the Blasintia (for that was what the Blasintium Texecs called themselves) was Kesc, and involved the moving of a number of objects across a board which was divided into squares.

The objects varied in shape and in the manner of their permitted movements. The idea was to remove the objects loyal to an opponent by occupying, with objects of one's own, the squares that they already occupied.

I assumed that the game was based on the real assumption that there was only so much room in a habitat, and that only a given number of people – each number being represented by one of the objects in the game – could occupy a given space at a given time.

This, I felt, was all very well. But there were always plenty of vacant spaces surrounding the objects, while in reality there was no vacant space anywhere.

The game was thus so far removed from life that at first I regarded it as sterile, accepting out of politeness only the male Edomand's invitation to play.

But I quickly developed an interest, and discovered that the mental exercise it offered was invaluable.

One evening the male Edomand and I were playing this game, with the female sitting by us, drawing different coloured threads through a coarse material to form a pattern, when he paused in the middle of a move and said: 'Why should they want you to go back to Cubale?'

I jumped, and knocked over some of the pieces. I apologised, and fussed over them, but the game was ruined.

'Who wants me to go back?' I asked.

'I don't quite know who, or even if,' he said. 'Someone in Cubale was asking us if we'd a stranger here. The des-

154

cription sounded just like you. It seems they want to talk to you.'

'And what did you tell them?'

'Oh. I didn't speak to them. It was someone else, over the videophone. But he told me about it, so I thought I'd ask you. Do you want to go back, by the way?'

'No, I don't think so.'

'Hmm. There are some strange things happening in Cubale, by all accounts. Anything to do with you?'

I began to tell him, but seeing that he was not really interested, gave up. Why was it that they would never listen to what I had to say even when it was in reply to their questions? It was almost as though they did not want to hear, and created a deafness within themselves as the occasion suited.

'I won't have to go back, will I?'

His hearing appeared to have been restored.

'Shouldn't think so,' he said. 'But it's not impossible.'

I could get no more from him about the mysterious call from Cubale, so in the end I gave up trying to find out. I could not see how I could be returned unless they sent me by force, which was not in the nature of the Blasintia. If a party of Cubale Texecs came to get me they would have to find me first, and I had the feeling that the Blasintia would hide me well, if I wished, despite their apparent indifference.

It was not the thought of pursuit by Magnon that worried me; it was my haunting by something else. Once I had developed the sense that a mysterious being was observing me I became obsessed by it.

The fact that no one else seemed to notice this strange presence made matters worse. I could never escape the thought that I was being watched, even when I was alone in my room.

It was in my room, in fact, that I felt I came closest to identifying the observer. I was reading a treatise about the old world when something made me look up at the wall. There, on the edge of the transparent section, was a pair of eyes close in, as though trying to beat the one-way opacity. Whether they could see through or not I could not tell, but for an instant those eyes and mine met.

The feeling this encounter gave me was uncanny; nevertheless I noted their shape and their faded colour and the way they looked so that I could recognise them again, then I ran from the room to the main door, opened it and went into the corridor outside.

There in the middle distance was the old man again, simply sitting and staring, his face in shadow. I decided to approach him, hesitated, went indoors, changed my mind. went out again – and he had gone.

I was surprised that he should have vanished so quickly, for he did not give the impression that he could walk at any pace, if at all. I was also surprised to see that at the place where he had been sitting there was no seat.

I spoke later to the Edomands about my experience but as so often happened their expressions turned blank as I developed my story, so I did not bother to finish.

I noticed though that when they thought I was not looking they exchanged a glance, and I was not surprised when they left the room together. I could hear them talking together somewhere in the apartment and after a while the male Edomand left.

She and I spent the rest of the day playing Kesc. For the first time, I won. But it gave me little pleasure.

The male Edomand returned shortly before bedtime. Once again there was a glance between him and his wife which I was not supposed to see. He asked me to be sure to remain in the apartment for the next day or two, and bade me goodnight.

I slept uneasily. Was this the end for me? Why should I be asked to remain in the apartment? Was it because the Blasintia had agreed to have me sent back to Cubale, and Magnon's men were coming to escort my return? Or was it because the Edomands knew that there was danger in the offing, and wanted me to be protected in their home?

Should I leave for another place, where there might be more danger, or should I stay in Blasintium and sit it out?

The latter course appealed to me because for some reason that I could not specify I was unable to believe that the Edomands would betray me lightly and, anyway, I was tired of running.

So I stayed put. But it was impossible to relax.

The next day the Edomands and I kept up our customary distant familiarity, but the atmosphere in the apartment had changed. They seemed apprehensive, as though they were expecting someone to call, and their apparent anxiety transferred itself to me and was multiplied fourfold.

By the time the old man came I was in a state approaching terror.

The door to my room swung quietly open and he was sitting there in the passageway outside. The male Edomand was with him. Then Edomand walked away and the old man came towards me.

The chair hissed quietly as it travelled over the floor.

13

SEEING my expression the old man smiled. 'I've no legs,' he said. 'That's why I must use this.' He pressed a little lever and the chair stopped and lowered itself half an inch to the ground.

I looked into his face. I recognised the eyes.

'It was you,' I said. 'All the time it was you. Here and in Cubale, even in Lemington.'

He nodded. 'I didn't want you to notice,' he said. 'I've been observing you all the time. In fact it was I who arranged for you to stay here. The authorities would have sent you back otherwise. The Edomands agreed to look after you for me, because I did not want you to know about me until I was absolutely sure.'

'Sure?' I repeated. 'Sure of what?'

He told me.

The next day at the prearranged hour I stood by the fountain and greenery in the main square which had so taken my attention when I first arrived in Blasintium and remained quite still as I had been told, while the people gathered round.

As they came in, rapidly filling the square, I reflected once more upon the great beauty of the Blasintia with their elegant bearing and comely manner of dress.

Observing them this time as one apart from the mass though I felt that there was a sort of heaviness about them, a lack of animation which made them resemble a gathering of wonderful machines more than a collection of individual beings.

Then momentarily I saw them as a unified conglomerate of bright cloth and flesh which swayed and swirled in my vision. I blinked my eyes and shook my head and looked at them again. I saw then that they were as one: there was the same expression of dull expectancy upon every face before me.

'Ahh!' Thousands of throats uttered simultaneously as the old man made his way through them, the cushions of air beneath his chair scarcely making a sound. The white robes falling from his shoulders trailed behind him and brushed softly past various members of the crowd, who moaned softly when they were touched.

He came up to the fountain and halted. His chair rotated slowly and as his gaze fell upon them the people sighed and closed their eyes and swayed about.

After some minutes of this, his chair ceased its rotary movement and lifted him into the air. He sat there some ten feet from the ground, his arms outstretched, his robes hanging so that he appeared to be perched upon some lofty and ephemeral support.

By now it seemed that the Blasintia had lost their hold upon reality. Most of them were seated upon the floor, eyes closed, swaying, humming discordantly. Some frothed at the mouth.

'Oto,' he said quietly.

'Mobilee,' they responded.

'Donor,' he intoned.

'Donor,' they confirmed.

This was repeated many times with variations of intensity and pitch. As the ritual progressed, the Blasintia became more engrossed in it. I had never dreamed that individuals would be capable of such absorption into the mass. They moved and uttered in total unison; it was hard to distinguish one from the other so uniform was their demeanour.

I found myself fascinated by them. As they swayed it seemed to me that I swayed with them.

'Oto,' said the old man.

'Mobilee,' they responded.

'Donor,' he intoned.

'Donor,' we confirmed.

'Phillips!'

The sound of my name was like a slap in the face. He looked down at me, furious.

'OK. Throw the switch.'

'The switch, the switch!' he hissed.

Oh, yes. Er, just there ...

The little button was where he had said it would be. I punched it.

Immediately the water stopped spouting from the statue. The oblong shape swung downwards and came to rest upon its four discs.

Just then the oblong uttered a growling and started to move forward slowly. The Blasintia in its way stood aside to allow its passage.

I stood there, transfixed, not looking at the oblong. The

sky was beginning to crack. Not right across but just up a little way starting from the horizon before me.

And as the blackness in it broadened I saw the Blasintia's beloved sky for the optical trick that it was: a mere roof, cunningly constructed and perfectly maintained but erected nevertheless for the purpose of illusion.

Then the screaming started. Somehow I had known that it would come.

First one, then two, then six wretched creatures staggered out. Naked, emaciated, greyish-white in colour, half blind, they groped uncertainly in the light of the square, seeking each other and huddling close when they found themselves, crying and moaning. They had stopped the screaming. But their backs were bleeding still from the whip-marks.

The oblong moved forward on its discs with the smoothness of a trolley, making the Blasintia scatter. But the creatures from the crack stood still as it bore down upon them. Only when it was too late did they make any attempt to avoid it.

One of them it missed at first. But by certain manoeuvrings it eventually trapped the maladroit and sluggish quarry into a corner. As it bore down upon the creature I closed my eyes. But that failed to shut out the shriek.

The oblong went backwards and forwards, pointing the discs on the front this way and that when it wanted to change direction. Almost graceful, it went over the prone bodies until they were flattened and beaten completely out of human shape.

Without waiting to see more I ran forward to the crack and bracing myself, looked in.

I don't know what it was that I had expected to see: I suppose I had prepared myself for a shock.

I looked into a chamber furnished with items that aroused longings and stirred long-lost memories. Small chairs and benches and tables were distributed throughout. Devices for rocking, wheeled things for rolling, laid about. A small idealised distorted replica of a human being lay pink on the floor. Scarcely knowing what I did, I picked it up and held it tight to me. Three of the walls were hung with crude, bold drawings, and before me was a thing that I found most evocative of all: fundamentally it was a flat tongue of plastic resting with its centre hinged upon a triangular support. I felt my lips moving. 'Cease,' I said, and: 'Sore.' Then: 'Cease-Sore, Ceasore, seasor, seesor, seesar, seesaw, seesaw.' I remember uttering these words without knowing their meaning to this day.

It was a strange room. Its fourth wall was apparently absent, and let on to a void. But gradually, as my eyes became used to peering into the gloom the void filled itself with horror.

I was ill prepared for what I saw. Those hundreds – maybe thousands of inert and almost faceless beings stretched out in lines running in all directions to disappear into tunnels of infinite blackness.

Now and then one of them stirred, or pulled at the wires leading from his scalp. I found their complete silence very strange – until I realised that I was looking at them through glass.

I stepped back, and walked out of the chamber, my mind a turmoil, just as the crack began to close. I remember feeling ashamed that the contents of the chamber moved me more than the pitiable sight that lay beyond it.

When the crack had disappeared the sky of the Blasintia assumed once again its limitless aspect, to the perfect illusion rejoiced in by the inhabitants.

Once it had given me pleasure, too.

I looked around and saw that the crowd was dispersing. The oblong, its bloody task completed, was back once more upon its plinth.

The bodies had gone, and no trace of their destruction remained. The Blasintia's garbage disposal had done its work as well as ever.

Weary and sick I made my way back to the Edomand residence. There was no solace there, but there was no place else to go.

Edomand greeted me at the door and let me in. I was surprised to see that he was wearing the same robes as I – I had not noticed him at the ceremony.

'Your thoughts are plain,' he said. 'But such worship is what they crave. In exchange for providing it he can do or have what he wishes. It sickens him, too, but he is prepared to countenance evil to achieve an ultimate good. Are not you, too?'

There was a pleading to his tone. Edomand spoke to me almost as a suppliant. I looked at him in a moment of wonderment, shook my head and, unable to speak, went to my room.

The old man had said that what I would see at the ceremony, standing by his side, would strengthen my resolve as it always strengthened his. I had replied at that time that my resolution was absolute, though I knew as I lay in my room afterwards that I had been wrong. But it was absolute now.

I slept for a while, then rose, bathed, dressed, ate and sealed the room in preparation for my mission.

Continuing to obey his instructions, I obtained the pointed metal bar that he said I would find in the cupboard, discovered the crack that lay between floor and wall, inserted the point and levered.

Slowly at first and then more easily the floor peeled upwards. After a while I was able to crook my fingers over the edge and I pulled strongly.

With a tearing noise the floor came away from its supports and left a gap sufficient for me to get through. Taking the flashlamp he had left me, I eased myself through the gap feet first and eased myself through.

Inch by inch I lowered myself down until my feet touched flesh. Its owner was too deeply unconscious to care.

I shone the beam in every direction. I was in a chamber from which led four passages. The floor was covered with comatose and naked Sleepees, lying head to feet. They stretched for as far as you could see along the passages in the beam of the lamp. And you knew more lay beyond. And more beyond them.

Blasintium was built on top of a network of cellars. And the cellars contained permanently unconscious Sleepees, automatically fed and cleansed and automatically sent for reprocessing upon expiry.

On the wall of the chamber there was a cupboard. I opened it and found the oxygen cylinder and mask, and the bag of tools that he said I would see there. I donned the mask and switched on the cylinder. I went back to the gap in the floor and closed it.

Then I set off on my quest, treading reluctantly at first, but then with less care on the living footway.

The walk was not long in fact, but it seemed to go on for an immense time. Sometimes the Sleepees thinned out and I was able to step between their bodies on to the floor, but for much of the time I had to walk upon them, and this was exhausting both mentally and physically.

All around me was blackness. My lamp was the only source of light. It was not surprising that the Texecs of Blasintium could live so well if they lavished so few of their resources upon the totally undemanding Sleepees under them.

I quelled the sense of hatred that arose in me.

Blame was equally to be shared, the old man had told me. The ascendancy of Texec over Sleepee was the direct result of the system established by the forebears of both, when mankind first left the outer world to escape his own pollution.

Men had graduated from living in air-conditioned houses to air-conditioned cities, with great roofs over them to keep out the poisoned atmosphere.

They found that only synthetically produced foods and reprocessed sewage water were fit to consume.

Eventually the air-conditioned cities were linked by air-conditioned highways and later by vacuum-filled tubes through which rockets could pass rapidly.

The inhabitants of the earth outside the cities fought to

enter the privileged places, which dug themselves deeper and deeper into the ground, and strengthened their canopies again and again against the covetous outsiders, for the artificial ecologies developed were capable of sustaining only a limited number. There was never enough room for all the earth's inhabitants in the air-conditioned cities and eventually those left outside became enfeebled and went into a decline in the foul open air, and grew incapable of building more cities for themselves.

For the first century or so, the remainder of mankind flourished in his artificial environment, but then suffered melancholy.

The city fathers called in all the experts in mind manipulation, and were persuaded by the advertising agencies that their techniques of artificially-induced dreaming, which they had begun to develop in the late twentieth century, could be turned to other uses than those of salesmanship.

The authorities agreed, and the custody of the race was delivered into the hands of the account executive. Dreams of the nature it had left were to restore the human spirit's equilibrium.

And so began the establishment of the dream-making élite. The élite strove to become more élite and the governed demanded only more insulation from reality, and that was all that they got.

So I could see that, as the old man had said, hatred of the Texec was sterile.

But a desire to eliminate him was not. It was this desire, a desire to change the order of things, that counted above all else, the old man said. And he had perceived that this desire burned deep and unquenchable within me.

I had followed his directions with great care. I had come to the end of the tunnel, as he said I would, and I was standing in a lofty, cylindrical chamber which tallied exactly with his description, except that it was smaller in diameter than he had remembered, and there was no door.

14

'No door?' he said, after my wearisome journey back to the Edomands where he was waiting for me. 'But there must be. I remember it well. I *know* it is there!'

I could understand that he would remember it well, but there was no shaking my conviction that I had seen no door.

He complained loud and long, using words that I did not understand, and cursed his chair that could not carry him along the corridors.

'Are you sure it was the right chamber?' I asked, and gave him details once more of the route I had taken.

'It must have been. It must have been.'

'Well, it wasn't really big enough to hold a door,' I said.

'Big enough or not, the door was there,' he said.

Then we spoke together: 'How big was it?'

He held his arms wide apart; I placed my hands at a distance of about three feet from one another.

'That's the answer then,' he said.

Wearily, I picked up hammer and chisel from the tool kit, put on my oxygen mask and lowered my way through the floor once again.

Once I got to the chamber again, I was able to find out where the door was by tapping the wall all round the chamber, and listening for it when it sounded different.

Some Texec overlord had decided that Blasintium was insufficiently insulated from the outer world for his safety, and had covered the opening with several feet of plastic.

It was now for me to hack his cover away.

I began enthusiastically enough, but after several hours had made a hole so small that it mocked my exhaustion.

Again I reported failure to the old man. 'It will take years at this rate,' I said. 'It's too tough.'

He nodded. 'You stay here awhile,' he said. 'I'll think of something.'

His invalid chair hissed softly as he withdrew from the room and went out into the corridors.

Edomand came into my room. 'He says you're to take these down to the chamber and come straight back here,' he said. He gave me a dozen pointed pick-hammers, tied together with some sort of line.

I lifted them, staggered under the weight a little, pulled up the floor once more and descended to the basements once again. Before my head went below the surface I looked at Edomand.

It was as though I had never seen him before. 'What's your part in all this?' I demanded.

He just smiled and shook his head.

Staggering along the by now familiar route, treading on the bruises my feet had caused the time before, I wished I knew more about what I was doing.

But the old man had told me that to know all now would be dangerous both for me and for our prospects of achieving change in the world.

Supposing, he argued, I were to tell what I knew under duress to someone like Magnon. He would make sure that no one would follow me. He liked the system the way it was, as the Texec overlord who sealed the door had. This gave him his power.

Thinking of that great skin of plastic over the old man's door, I was persuaded to discipline my curiosity. But it was still annoying to be kept in ignorance.

Panting in my oxygen mask I arrived at the chamber. A Sleepee, standing, turned to stare at me with sightless eyes. Treading delicately over the wires that fell from his cranium to the floor and thence to the corridor, he came up to me and took the picks from me.

He undid the line and let eleven of the picks fall to the floor, retaining one in his hands. He walked over to the section of plastic that I had attacked, and smote it with an unbelieveable force.

I staggered back, stunned by the noise. His strength was prodigious.

Fascinated yet appalled by this display of power I ran back along the corridor, tripping over the bodies as the enormous sound of steel biting into plastic pursued me.

Edomand was waiting in my room for me. 'He says you're to come with me,' he said, and without waiting for me to recover my breath went out of the room expecting me to keep up with him.

He took me to a part of Blasintium I had not seen before. Although the air was still perfectly sweet and rich, the corridors were meaner, less well lit and poorly furnished.

'Here,' he said, and turned into a doorway.

'Come in, Phillips,' said the old man. 'You ought to watch this.' He indicated the screen in front of him, and then waved me to a chair beside him.

On the screen was the image of the chamber I had left. The perspective was as though I were seeing it through my own eyes. Suddenly a pair of arms swung into the picture. It was as though they were swinging from a pair of shoulders placed each side of and slightly below the screen. The hands were holding one of those picks. The point of the pick struck the plastic firmly, and the fault, already large, grew larger still.

'You're looking at it through the eyes of a Sleepee. It's a feedback from the dream machine,' he said. 'I've induced artificial somnambulism, and can make him do what I want.' He smiled wanly at me.

'Then why haven't you used this method before?'

'Two reasons, mainly. One you will learn in a minute. And the other – there's no point in sending a Sleepee through that door. There's a long way to go after you get through, and the wires simply aren't long enough. Anyway, when he goes up there – as you will learn – a man has to be able to think for himself.'

The image on the screen went blurred, then blank.

'And that's the other reason,' said the old man. 'Now

he's dead.' The image reappeared. 'And here comes another one.'

'He's going to die, too?'

The old man nodded. 'Oh yes. I'm having to get them to use all their reserves to attack that wall. And their reserves are pretty low. That's why I wanted you . . . oh, well, never mind.'

I could see that he was upset. So would I have been. Killing people, even permanently unconscious Sleepees, was not something to be undertaken lightly.

'Maybe they would have been willing to die if they'd been able to make the decision themselves,' I said.

'In fact I picked out a dozen who are suffering from sleepstate phobias. So they were desperate. Locked in night-mare, with no escape such as you had.'

'I see. But how come you know all this?'

He smiled a bitter half smile. 'As high priest I know many things. I have many ways of finding out what I need to know and I have caused much pain in my discovery. That's why you must succeed – so that all the pain is not wasted.'

The change of subject was abrupt, but it revealed to me the power of his obsession.

I thought to myself for a while and envisaged the millions making their way to freedom and then asked: 'If we do breach a way to the outer world, and everyone does get out, eventually – will there be enough room?'

He looked at me gravely. 'More than enough,' he said. 'The outside world is immeasurably bigger than these little hutches in which we now live. There are far fewer people outside than in. At least there were . . . .'

He shook his head ruefully. 'I never guessed what I would find when I first discovered that tunnel. Just think! Two peoples, one subterranean, one on the surface, each having forgotten the existence of the other.'

'How could that happen?'

He shrugged. 'I don't know. I wasn't around when it did happen. But I guess the people who survived above ground

– people, mostly who lived a long way from big population centres – were too bothered about their own survival to worry too much about history. They just came in from their remote islands, or from the tundra or the desert or whatever remote region they inhabited, to find that the great temperate continents were empty of people. They didn't ask why, they just accepted it. After all, the underground emigration had happened several generations ago by the time these people discovered Europe and America and Asia again.'

I understood less than half of what he said. But I felt that I would never forget his words. And I never have, and now I understand them.

'You see, as soon as advanced man left the surface of the earth, it began to recover. The filth was washed from the sky by great rains, and was not replaced. It was absorbed in the ground and in the water by certain specialised plantlife of the sea and the earth which flourished on the muck, was specially adapted by nature to do so, and was at last allowed to undertake its assigned task.

'For a time this plantlife prospered in the absence of artificial controls, but when all the pollutants had been absorbed by them and neutralised and returned once more to the earth, the other plants returned – the grasses and the trees which had succoured man in his feebleness and which he killed in his greed.'

'Greed,' I said. 'Will we not make the place foul again with these industries when we go back up to it? Or do you hope that we shall see that it is beautiful and clean and try to keep it so?'

He laughed, but again without mirth.

'I'm not hoping that you will change human nature merely by showing the race its birthplace,' he said. 'It's altogether more practical than that – it is simply a matter of survival. The machines of the underground world, wrought by those ingenious and suicidal humans who once lived upon the upper world, are finally coming to the end of their life. The rate of their decline is accelerating, and there is neither the wit nor the materials to replace them. The world that you know is leaking, and its resources are being irretrieveably lost.'

Still the screen told us that a somnambulist Sleepee was hacking a way through to the door. The picture faded and died with the expiry of the Sleepee and blossomed into light again as another took his place.

'With the standards of retention in decline, so the production of reprocessed consumables declines, and with that the population itself must tend to decline as well, one way or another.'

'By letting the Sleepees die out,' I said.

'Just so. The sacrifice you saw is a symbol of the necessity. But with any decline in population the supply of waste diminishes and so on. A process of progressive division is under way. For example, once the Sleepees are gone the Texecs could continue for perhaps four generations, provided that each generation was smaller than its predecessor. And after that, only a handful of scavengers could be supported.'

The flickering screen above us continued to show the labours of a doomed Sleepee. The image went blurred and then went blank for an instant as he blinked the sweat from his eyes and then it came clear again.

'The inhabitants of the world as you know it are the unwitting victims of a vast technical decay. And this decay is a result of initial spiritual unpreparedness in the race for subterranean living centuries ago. They were infinitely ingenious in providing themselves with a bolt hole to escape the results of their folly – and as infinitely inept in dealing with the folly itself. Technical geniuses – spiritual idiots.' He grimaced. 'And now we've come full circle – nearly.'

He was talking on a scale above and beyond my imagination. In the effort to follow his words I had forgotten the most important part of his story. Then I remembered.

'What about me?'

'Ah, you. As I said, I chose you. Not just you of course

but all the others failed. I sent you your dream at the outset to show you the rewards of the outer world and the penalties for failing to attain it. Others have already paid the penalty in their despair. The reward is now within your grasp . . .'

His fingers clawed the air before my face. Behind them his eyes blazed. Then the fire went out of them. He placed the hand upon his lap and his shoulders slumped a little. He seemed to draw within himself and fell into repose.

Then he looked up at me and smiled. 'You will get there because you must,' he said softly. 'You have nothing to fear. You are a formidable being, a hero, Phillips. And it is I who have made you thus.'

'You?'

He nodded. 'Of course. I could control this world down here. I can do whatever I like in Blasintium, and my freedom is almost complete elsewhere.'

'But the Texecs . . .'

He smiled again. 'They're a simple folk. Those who know me well – and I make sure that they are few but important – think of me almost as a god. They don't know why they think of me thus, but I know.'

'Why?'

He seemed to be about to reply and then to change his mind. He looked back at the screen.

Perhaps if he had continued talking I would have understood his words there and then, instead of having to wait a decade for comprehension. But there was no time then for more explanations. Perhaps it was as well.

But I had no time to think about this. At that moment the male Edomand came into the dreamfeed unit. He glanced at the screen for several seconds before speaking to me. He looked worried.

'There's someone arrived from Cubale looking for you,' he said. 'She says it's very important. So I took her home and came to find you. Do you think she means trouble? Should I tell her you've left, or what?'

Her. It had to be Gnofina. 'Is she on her own?'

'Oh, yes.'

Then she couldn't do much harm. Not if I am careful. And she might have something useful to tell.

'Shall I go?' I asked the old man.

'You haven't much time,' he said. 'They're nearly through.'

I said: 'I shan't lose much time if I do see her.'

'All right.' He gave me the instructions once more, and said goodbye.

He turned back to the controls and called in the tenth Sleepee.

Edomand and I hurried back to his apartment. She was sitting in the main room, looking thinner and older. She came over to me and kissed me. The Edomands left the room.

'I forgive you,' she said.

'What for?'

'That girl. I'd come to the tubeport to arrange your escape – and then I find you there with her. I could have killed you then.'

'But you didn't stop the tuberocket . . . though you did get some men to arrest me.'

She smiled. 'Not very consistent, I suppose. I didn't know whether I wanted you to get away or to be imprisoned for the rest of your life, so I thought I would let it be decided by chance.'

'And a man died as a result.'

'I realised then how terribly wrong I had been. Right at that moment. I told them to let you go then, and I think they were pleased to. But I haven't slept well since.'

'I have.'

'That's because you've no personal feelings.'

'I *have*.'

She shook her head. 'Not proper feelings. All the Sleepees have been crippled emotionally, one way or the other. I know that now. It's not your fault. I mean . . . I love you, but you don't love me, and you never can.'

'Love?'

172

She came up to me. 'That's why I'm here. I've come to tell you that Magnon and some others are coming here for you. They've decided that so long as you are alive they will never be secure. There's Magnon, and a man from Lemington – Antonio, I think. So you must leave. They mean to kill you.'

'Well,' I said. 'Thanks.'

Her eyes clouded. 'Thanks,' she repeated. 'Oh, dear.'

For Magnon and Antonio to come to a foreign city just for me was flattering. Though it was a form of flattery I could do without.

'If they come here you'll be in trouble,' I said. 'You'd better come with me, Gnofina.'

We went to my room and prised up the floor. 'Come on,' I said, and dropped through. Hesitantly, she followed. I had forgotten to warn her about the subterranean Sleepees and she screamed when her foot landed on one.

'Never mind,' I said. 'He's used to it.'

I got my breathing apparatus from the cupboard and took out another one for her. With our masks fixed we walked along the path of flesh to the chamber. I was used to the route by now, but Gnofina found it gruelling.

By the time we got to the chamber, she was in tears.

The last of the Sleepees was there, hacking away at the remains of the plastic. His blows rang out and echoed against the walls. My ears sang, my head was filled with noise. Desperately I put my hands up to stop the sound and I saw that Gnofina had done the same.

Then, suddenly, it stopped. The Sleepee dropped the pick – there were only two unbroken ones remaining – turned away from the door. Walking stiffly, his eyes wide open and unblinking, he came towards us. I could see that there were tears running down his cheeks and then, something like a smile disturbed his face. He came towards us. Gnofina shrank against the wall. I stepped back and he passed us into the corridor.

Gradually I found that I could hear again. 'What's he

173

doing?' Gnofina was shouting at me. 'He's gone away to die,' I shouted back. My voice sounded tinny.

Then I heard the Sleepee's final shriek, triumphant upon discovering release. I took his pick in both hands and hacked away at the remaining lumps of plastic which still stuck to the door.

The final lump fell away and I took the locking wheel in both hands and tried to turn it. It would not budge, so I took up the pick again, inserted the handle between the spokes and tried to lever it round.

Still I could not shift it. 'You, too,' I told Gnofina and she got another pick and did the same as me. Together we strained against the time-stiffened lock. It was no use.

Then I picked up the largest lump of plastic that I could see and gradually, with Gnofina's help, lifted it above my head. Then I dashed it onto the pick head.

Miraculously, the handle did not break. Instead, the wheel shifted slightly. Again I brought the plastic down and again it moved.

Once more Gnofina and I tried to turn the wheel by leverage and this time, slowly, quarter-inch by quarter inch, we succeeded. 'Stop,' I said. 'Listen.'

There were voices somewhere back in the tunnel.

We looked at each other and redoubled our efforts. But our strength was going.

And then the wheel gave. I found that with only a little effort I could spin it. I spun and pulled, spun and pulled. The voices were coming nearer. I thought I recognised Magnon's. It was a small consolation to think that they would be finding the going extremely difficult.

15

THEN I pulled again and this time the door gave slightly on its hinges. There was a shrieking, and a blast of atmosphere from the other side struck me, pure and chill. I shivered and the sweat on my face went cold. I breathed in and I found something like fire running through my arteries.

Visions came to me, of open water and of islands and of strange fruit, of fleepers bouncing through the cornfields and orchards and over the top of the water. Was this what had been promised in my dreamstate, so long ago? Was there a whiff of it in this air that rushed about us?

The hinges were so stiff. I put the point of the pick in the crack and heaved again. The door was about a foot thick.

'Quick, quick,' whispered Gnofina harshly. As I paused for an instant I could hear the others grunting and cursing as they stumbled over the Sleepees on their way towards us.

One final effort, with me pulling on the handle and with Gnofina pushing, the door opened wide enough for us to squeeze through. I took a deep breath, removed my breathing apparatus.

'I'll go first,' I said. I edged myself through, panicking momentarily as the pick in my hand caught on some impediment. Then I turned round, grabbed Gnofina's hand and pulled. She just made it, but it hurt, I could tell by her face.

I tried to pull the door to. I managed to narrow the gap but could not shut it completely. I rammed the pick handle through the wheel which corresponded to the one on the other side, and eased it along so that one end overlapped the jamb. It was not much of a barrier, but it would at least delay them.

We stood for a moment. Even in our fear, we rejoiced in the air that swirled and tugged about us, coming down from above, to roar through the gap in the door into the low pressure of Blasintium's atmosphere.

It was heady stuff. Even then, at that moment, I laughed at my thoughts. Already the calculations by which the air-conditioners of Blasintium were run would be upset; doubtless the apparatus would be going berserk. Then I thought of the hermetic seals at the tubeport. How soon would they be breached? Would the Sleepees now be stirring as the rich clean air now washed over them? And what embarrassment would be caused to the languid, elegant Blasintia when they found themselves with a surplus of energy as a result of breathing this magnificent draught?

The air current gathered in intensity instead of diminishing; perhaps doors were being opened in Blasintium that had not been opened for years, and were easing the passage of this air from the outside world.

Gnofina shivered and came close to me.

'What is it?' she said. Suddenly I realised that she knew nothing of the outside. There was no time to tell her either.

'I'm tapping a new source of rich atmosphere. It's a limitless supply,' I said, using terms she might understand.

She asked no more questions.

'Phillips!'

The shout was like a whisper in the roaring of the air.

'Phillips!' It was Magnon.

We had to move. The door was stiff and the pickhandle strong, but the pressure of the air upon it would make it easier for them to open.

'Come on.' I took Gnofina's hand and together we stumbled across the little square space to the ladder that ran up the wall opposite. I was astonished at the speed with which she climbed the ladder, and then astonished myself at my own speed, too – despite the pressure of the air bearing down upon us.

Fifteen or twenty feet above the floor was a small gallery, with a door leading off. It was a flimsy affair compared with the main door below, and the cracks at the top and the bottom were letting through a draught that was almost solid: once, my feet were blown from under me.

'How do we open this?'

I shook my head. It seemed impossible, against that weight of air.

But I tried the handle, turned it, and shoved. I put my feet against the metal rails of the gallery and shoved again. It gave an inch, then slammed shut. Nothing could prevail against that pressure.

Then I had an idea. With my shoulders against the railings, I kicked at the door. Momentarily the metal gave way under my feet, caving slightly in. Then it bulged outwards towards us. Again and again I kicked and eventually was rewarded with the sight of light coming through a crack running across the metal where the constant kicking had weakened it. I kept on kicking it in, and the air kept on forcing it out again. 'Look out!'

I pulled myself to one side as the crack suddenly widened and tore. A tongue of metal stood out from the door, wagging up and down. The air howled through the crack in triumph at finding more release. The metal tongue broke away from the door and was carried rapidly below, where it hit the wall, point first, and stuck in. Slowly it bent and was flattened against the wall, where it remained.

More metal peeled back from the door. Objects from above would be dragged through the hole, tearing away more metal in their passage. From time to time I could help it out by crooking my fingers round a curl and pulling.

As the hole widened, so more air came down the tunnel beyond, through the gap in the door below and into the starved atmosphere of Blasintium.

But we were trapped, clinging to the gallery, one each side of the door.

Above the noise of the air there was another sound: a

great creaking which rose briefly to a shriek and culminated in a clanging sound, as though a huge metallic object had been hurled against a wall.

I shone my flashlamp down and saw that this was indeed what had happened: the air pressure had forced open the main door below, snapping the restraining pick handle. In the chamber beyond I could see two shapes – Magnon and Antonio – pressed against the wall. Somehow they were clinging on to that circular wall; possibly they were being helped by a trick of the airflow.

It was consoling, though, to think that while we were trapped up here, they were trapped down there. We were safe – so long as the gallery held firm.

The wind, released now from the impediment offered by the main door, redoubled its vigour again. The gap in our little door widened more and more rapidly, until it split from top to botton and the side opposite the hinges came completely away, striking the rails of the gallery and then spinning down to the chamber below and through.

The half-door smote the wall above Magnon's head and then fell to the floor before wafting almost idly into the corridor beyond. He did not flinch.

Suddenly I noticed a diminution in the rush of the air.

Below, I could see Magnon and Antonio struggling to move away from their wall. I looked at Gnofina.

'Can you move?' I simply mouthed the words. Giving utterance to them would have been a waste of time. Her face was slightly distorted by the pressure against it. She nodded.

Inch by inch, clinging to whatever solid objects we could find, we eased through the door.

I looked back and could see that Antonio and Magnon were doing the same below. The pursuit had started again.

Before us was a concrete area and we were faced once again with doors – a pair of double doors on which was painted in large letters of white, pitted here and there with brown spots and streaks, the word 'ELEVATOR'.

To one side of these doors was a flight of steps. I pointed

to them and Gnofina started to walk, then to crawl towards them. On our hands and knees we went, offering as little resistance to the airstream as possible. The steps had a railing each side and we pulled on this with our hands and pushed against the steps with our feet to achieve progress.

As we turned the first corner I glanced back and caught a glimpse, I thought, of a hand gripping the door lintel, preparatory to pulling its owner through from the gallery.

And if I had seen correctly, they were gaining on us.

Then it seemed to me that our progress was becoming increasingly easy. The noise of the wind was diminishing still more. The pressure against our faces was lessening. We forced our way upwards, almost running, then two steps at a time.

Our breath came in great gasps as we made our way up the stairs, winding upwards, upwards endlessly it seemed. The sound of the wind had fallen enough for us to hear our pursuers' footfalls behind us on the stairs.

I found myself almost longing for the wind to strike down again. For one of the great hermetic seals in the world below to give way and for the air to be sucked in from above once more.

I could hear the two others breathing behind me, but I dared not look round. Suddenly I sensed that Gnofina was no longer with me. Then I heard Magnon shout and I heard her voice, too. There was the sound of a scuffle, and a blow, and a scream. Then respite, as I continued the climb.

Then the sound of pursuit was resumed, but it was less close behind. One day I would repay Gnofina but first I had to get away from Magnon.

The stairs came to an end.

They led into a passageway at the end of which was a pair of swing doors which once had been glazed. They were half open, being held in that position by the incoming wind.

I ran towards them, staggering from side to side of the passage as I went.

179

'Stop!'

It was Magnon. I tried to run faster but could not. I hoped he was as exhausted as I.

There was a cracking sound as something hit the floor behind me, then slithered past my heels. It was a pick. In desperation he had thrown it at me. I took it up as I ran.

I pushed through the doors and ran into a rough cave which itself led on to a narrow path. The exit was covered with a mass of hanging green things and I braved them and pushed them aside as I went through.

The roaring in my ears gave way to a kind of silence and the light blinded me.

Then in the silence I heard a sound which resolved itself into a multitude of sounds, tiny, new and full of promise.

Gradually I regained my vision. I was standing on top of a mound. Before me lay an infinity of green and brown surface and above was a ceiling of limitless blue. In the blue hung a disc too bright to look at and it warmed you like the simulated sun of Blasintia. Then across the face of this disc rode a great puff of grey, and I saw that here and there in the blue were other great puffs, with white rounded tops and flat grey bellies.

Below and far away, near to a wide shining stretch of water, some creatures hopped. I peered towards them but distance had eliminated details. They *could* be men on fleepers.

I began to run again.

My head began to reel, although my mind remained perfectly clear. I bethought me of the prodigious physical effort I had made by running, running against that great stream of air, up and up that enormous flight of stairs.

I realised then that I was still running, running faster than ever. I forced myself to stop, and stood upon shaking limbs. My breathing was shallow and my heart beat so quickly that one pulse almost merged with another, and instead of a pounding in my ears there was something like vibration. I felt no fatigue. In my exhilaration, I felt as though I could continue for ever.

180

I looked behind me. The cave, some hundreds of yards to my rear, was now concealed by the green stuff that hung in festoons before its mouth.

To my right and slightly in front of me was a tangled complex of green. I dived into it and screamed as the sharpness of it tore my flesh.

Then I lay there, breathing as little as I could. I knew that I had never breathed such as this before. The finest atmosphere – the hundred per cent as it was called – of the world below was meagre in comparison.

I peered out of my hiding place, scratching myself more as I did so, and saw the others emerge from the greenery covering the cave. First Magnon, then Antonio then, some way behind, Gnofina. My heart leaped upon seeing her and I restrained a gasp. Her face was bloody. It had been bloodied on my behalf and I knew then that I could love – did love – her. I forced myself to remain calm under the onrush of adrenalin.

Magnon staggered, paused as I had done, looked about him, shouted something at Antonio, and started running towards my hiding place. Antonio ran in another direction, his legs blurring with speed.

Gnofina stayed put. I prayed that she would remain still. She did.

Magnon pounded past my hiding place, down the slope. I stayed there, tolerating the excruciating discomfort of my sanctuary.

Then I heard my enemy's return up the slope. The ground shook under his mighty steps. I could see him approach. His eyes, wildly starting, swivelled in the magenta of his face.

It was time for the coup de grace.

I stood, and shouted his name. His progress ceased and he remained where he was. But he was unable to prevent his feet from continuing to rise and fall. As I watched him running on the spot I felt trickles of blood running down my leg. And then I saw the trickles of blood running from his nose, his ears, his eyes. Soon it was running down the insides of his legs, too.

Magnon's insides had burst.

I had heard of how an excess of oxygen could burn up a man – it had happened in Lemington once or twice when machines had gone wrong – but I had never seen it happening before.

Scarcely daring to breathe, I clambered from my hiding place and, walking as slowly as I could, stepped over the fallen Magnon, and made my way towards Gnofina. Stricken by a happy terror upon emerging from the cave into the day she had found that her limbs would not obey the dictates of her mind. She wanted to flee, but could not.

I embraced her and a shudder ran through her frame. Unspeaking, she pointed. Following her gaze I saw in the distance the prone form of Antonio.

'Dead,' I said. 'Magnon, too.'

She nodded.

Together we went down the stairs into the gallery, down the ladder to the great door that had taken so much to open.

Beyond the door lay the sound of a great murmuring and a screaming.

The sound was approaching.

Sadly I closed the door and made it fast.

They had to be prepared before they came out.

I would have to prepare them before they came out.

I would have to find a way.

I, and Gnofina, and those men on the fleepers.